H. Cholmondeley Pennell

The Muses of Mayfair

Selections from vers de société of the nineteenth century

H. Cholmondeley Pennell

The Muses of Mayfair
Selections from vers de société of the nineteenth century

ISBN/EAN: 9783743359826

Manufactured in Europe, USA, Canada, Australia, Japa

Cover: Foto ©Andreas Hilbeck / pixelio.de

Manufactured and distributed by brebook publishing software (www.brebook.com)

H. Cholmondeley Pennell

The Muses of Mayfair

U

CHATTO AN

TO FREDERICK LOCKER.

DEAR LOCKER! whom I knew unknown, but now
    Known wheresoe'er rhyme runs or critics carp,—
    None strikes a clearer, more melodious harp
        Than thou.

Thine is the spell that charms alike the sage,
    Craving repose for wearied brain and eye,
    And the fair child lingering her play-hour by
        Thy page.

No vulgar lures, no tinsel arts are thine
    To gild the common coarseness of the herd—
    Still be thyself, unblamed in thought or word,
        And shine.

And for the lustre of thy name I hold
    Twice dear, old friend, this gleaned and garnered sheaf,
    Which thence shall gain one doubly-treasured leaf
        Of gold.

H. C. P.

NOTE BY THE EDITOR.

THE greater part of the poems in this collection are copyright, and are presented by the very kind and courteous permission of their authors and publishers. A few—including the translations at the end of the volume—have not appeared before in print.

H. CHOLMONDELEY PENNELL.

LONDON, *May* 1874.

CONTENTS.

TRANSLATIONS FROM THE FRENCH AND GERMAN

By Ethel Grey.

"*BEAUTY CLARE.*"

[*Extract.*]

Hamilton Aïdé.

HALF Lucrece, half Messalina,
    Lovely piece of Sèvres china,
        When I see you, I compare
You with common, quiet creatures,
Homely delf in ways and features—
            Beauty Clare !

Surely Nature must have meant you
For a Syren, when she sent you
        That sweet voice and glittering hair :
—Was it touch of human passion
Made you woman, in a fashion—
            Beauty Clare ?

I think not.   The moral door-step
Cautiously you never o'er-step
    When your victims you ensnare—
—Lead them on with hopes—deceive them—
Then turn coldly round, and leave them,
            Beauty Clare.

Some new slave I note each season,
Wearing life away, his knees on
    (Moths around the taper's flare!)
Guardsman fine,—or young attaché,
Black and smooth as papier-maché;
            Beauty Clare.

In your box I see them dangling,
Triumphs of successful angling,
    Trophies ranged behind your chair;
How they watch the fan you flutter!
How they drink each word you utter,
            Beauty Clare!

When at kettle-drums presiding,
I admire your tact, dividing
    Smiles to each, in equal share,
Lest one slave wax over-jealous,
Or another grow less zealous,
          Beauty Clare !

What perfection in your waltzing !
How in vain the women all sing,
    When you warble some sweet air !
But, your sentimental ditty
Over,—you are then the witty
          Beauty Clare.

How you light the smouldering embers
Of decrepit Peers and Members !
    While you still have smiles to spare
For a new-fledged boy from college,
Sitting at *your* feet for knowledge !
          —Beauty Clare !

At your country seat in Salop,
What contention for a gallop
    With you, on your chestnut mare !
How the country-misses hate you,
Seeing o'er a five-barred gate,—you,
        Beauty Clare !

All-accomplished little creature !
Fatally endowed by nature,—
    Were your inward soul laid bare,
What should we discover under
That seductive mask, I wonder,
        Beauty Clare ?

EQUES SOLITARIUS.

HAMILTON AÏDÉ.

I RODE in the bright spring weather,
   'Neath the hawthorn's budding branch,
   In my doublet of Spanish leather,
  And beside me Lady Blanche.
The birds sang out their love songs,
   The young leaves slipped their sheaths,—
I—only I—on Hope's gay stream
   Flung out no fragrant wreaths.

I thought that she loved another—
   "And how," with scorn I cried,
"She will barter her true heart's treasure
   For the grace of my acres wide!"

So I never trusted her blushes,
   Nor the smile of her gracious lips,
And I steeled my heart, as I bent my face,
   And touched her finger-tips.

And oft in the years that followed,
   When Blanche was past away,
I rode 'neath those budding hawthorns
   With damoisels fair and gay.
But even through song and laughter,
   I heard my sad heart sigh
Too late, for the priceless treasure,
   That I had thrown, careless, by !

WINFRED'S HAIR.

Hamilton Aïdé.

WINFRED, waking in the morning,
  Locks dishevelled, sighed, " Alas !
Broken is the Venice-bodkin
That you gave me—'twas of glass.
All my auburn hair, henceforward,
  Shall be given to the wind."
Ere the evening came, another's
  Net of pearls her hair confined.

Frail as the Venetian bauble
  I had thrust in Winfred's hair,
Lo ! the net now snapped asunder
  Other hands had fastened there ;

Ere the moon's wide-blossomed petals
　　On the breast of night had died,
Net and bodkin both deserted,
　　Winfred's glittering hair flowed wide !

Silver comb and silken fillet
　　Next, in turn, the wild hair bound,
Till, at length, the crown of wifehood
　　Clasped its hands that hair around.
Golden crown of Love ! displacing
　　Girlhood's vain adornments there,
Winfred never more shall alter,
　　Now, the fashion of her hair.

A BUNCH OF VIOLETS.

HAMILTON AÏDÉ.

HERE is the bunch of violets
　　She crushed in her ivory palm,
The night she beheld that fair-haired girl
　　On Reginald Ashton's arm.

They can tell no secrets :
　　They can never betray
How the passionate heart, in that hour,
　　Burnt to its core away.

For, as upon grass a circle
　　Marks where the fire hath been,
In her heart of hearts are ashes,
　　Where dew once fed the green.

But the violets tell no secrets ;
  They in the old desk lie,
'Mong bundles of yellow letters,
  Where they were flung to die.

She never reads the letters,
  Nor touches the withered leaves ;
She never looks behind her,
  Nor over the dead past grieves.

Vigilant, keen and active,
  With ready, helpful hands,
To lift the burthen from others,
  In the world's highway she stands.

But all the romance of girlhood,
  The youth-time of hope and pride,
Were swept away the evening
  That bunch of violets died !

ON AN INTAGLIO HEAD OF MINERVA.

THOMAS BAILEY ALDRICH.

THE cunning hand that carved this face,
   A little helmeted Minerva—
The hand, I say, ere Phidias wrought,
Had lost its subtle skill and fervour.

Who was he? Was he glad or sad?
   Who knew to carve in such a fashion?
Perchance he shaped this dainty head
   For some brown girl that scorned his passion.

But he is dust: we may not know
   His happy or unhappy story:
Nameless and dead these thousand years,
   His work outlives him—there's his glory!

Both man and jewel lay in earth
　　Beneath a lava-buried city;
The thousand summers came and went,
　　With neither haste, nor hate, nor pity.

The years wiped out the man, but left
　　The jewel fresh as any blossom.
Till some Visconti dug it up,
　　To rise and fall on Mabel's bosom.

O Roman brother! see how Time
　　Your gracious handiwork has guarded;
See how your loving, patient art
　　Has come, at last, to be rewarded.

Who would not suffer slights of men,
　　And pangs of hopeless passion also,
To have his carven agate-stone
　　On such a bosom rise and fall so!

SAINT MAY:

A CITY LYRIC.

J. ASHBY-STERRY.

ST ALOYS the Great is both mouldy and grim,
   The decalogue's dusty, the windows are dim;
     Not knowing the road there, you'll long have
        to search
To find your way into this old City church;
Yet on fine Sunday mornings I frequently stray
There to see a new saint, whom I've christened St May.

Of saints I've seen plenty in churches before—
In Florence or Venice they're there by the score;
Agnese, Maria—the rest I forget—
By Titian, Bassano, and brave Tintoret:

They none can compare, though they're well in their
    way,
In maidenly grace with my dainty St May.

She's young for a saint, for she's scarcely eighteen,
And ne'er could wear peas in those dainty *bottines;*
Her locks are not shaven, and 'twould be a
    sin
To wear a hair-shirt next that delicate skin;
Save diagonal stripes on a dress of light gray,
Stripes ne'er have been borne by bewitching St
    May.

Then she's almost too plump and too round for a
    saint,
With sweet little dimples that Millais might paint;
She has no mediæval nor mortified mien,
No wimple of yellow, nor background of green,
A nimbus of hair throws its sunshiny ray
Of glory around the fair face of St May.

What surquayne or partlet could look better than
My saint's curly jacket of black Astracan?
What coif than her bonnet—a triumph of skill—
Or alb than her petticoat edged with a frill?
So sober, yet smiling—so grave, yet so gay,
Oh, where is a saint like my charming St May?

PET'S PUNISHMENT.

J. ASHBY-STERRY.

OH, if my love offended me,
　　And we had words together,
　To show her I would master be,
　I 'd whip her with a feather !

If then she, like a naughty girl,
　　Would tyranny declare it,
　I 'd give my pet a cross of pearl,
　　And make her always bear it.

If still she tried to sulk and sigh,
　　And threw away my posies,
　I 'd catch my darling on the sly,
　　And smother her with roses !

But should she clench her dimpled fists,
  Or contradict her betters,
I 'd manacle her tiny wrists
  With dainty golden fetters.

And if she dared her lips to pout—
  Like many pert young misses—
I 'd wind my arm her waist about,
  And punish her—with kisses !

A BOAT-RACE SKETCH.

J. ASHBY-STERRY.

ON sorrow and joy she has seen the beginning—
  Her lightness of spirit half dashed by the
    "blues"—
With cheers in her heart for the crew who are winning,
  Whilst tears fill her eyes for those fated to loes.
If you'll narrowly watch 'midst the noise and contention,
  You 'll note, as her Arab paws proudly the dust,
A deftly-twined bouquet of speedwell and gentian
  'Neath her little white collar half carelessly thrust !
The tint of a night in the still summer weather
  Her tight-fitting habit just serves to unfold,

Whilst delicate cuffs are scarce fastened together
  By dainty-wrought fetters of turquoise and gold.
Ah, climax of sweet girlish neutral devices !
  What smiles for the winners, for losers what sighs !—
She has twined her fair hair with the colours of Isis,
  Whilst those of the Cam glitter bright in her eyes.

BLANCHE.

[*An Extract from "The Season."*]

ALFRED AUSTIN.

YOU knew Blanche Darley? could we but once
more
Behold that belle and pet of '54!
Not e'en a whisper, vagrant up to town
From hunt or race-ball, augured her renown.
Far in the wolds sequestered life she led,
Fair and unfettered as the fawn she fed:
Caressed the calves, coquetted with the colts,
Bestowed much tenderness on turkey poults:
Bullied the huge ungainly bloodhound pup,
Tiffed with the terrier, coaxed to make it up:

The farmers quizzed about the ruined crops,

The fall of barley, and the rise of hops:

Gave their wives counsel, but gave flannel too,

Present where'er was timely deed to do;

Known, loved, applauded, prayed for, far and wide—

The wandering sunshine of the country side.

So soft her tread, no nautilus that skims

With sail more silent than her liquid limbs.

Her hair so golden that, did slanting eve

With a stray curl its sunlight interweave,

Smit with surprise, you gazed, but could not guess

Which the warm sunbeam, which the warmer tress.

Her presence was low music; when she went,

She left behind a dreamy discontent,

As sad as silence when a song is spent.—

She came—we saw—were conquered: one and all

We donned the fetters of delicious thrall.

We fetched, we carried, waited, doffed, and did

Just as our Blanche the beautiful would bid.

Such crowds petitioned her at every ball

For "just one waltz," she scarce could dance at all!

Her card besieged with such intrigues and sighs,
It might have been the pass-book to the skies.
We lost our heads.   Have women wiser grown?
A marvel surely, had she kept her own !

L O S T.

ALFRED AUSTIN.

SWEET lark! that bedded in the tangled grass,
  Protractest dewy slumbers, wake, arise!
The brightest moments of the morning pass—
Thou shouldst be up, and carolling in the skies.
Go up! go up! and melt into the blue,
  And to heaven's veil on wings of song repair;
But, ere thou dost descend to earth, peep through,
  And see if she be there.

Sweet stockdove! cooing in the flushing wood,
  On one green bough brooding till morn hath died,
Oh, leave the perch where thou too long hast stood,
  And with strong wings flutter the leaves aside!

Fly on, fly on, past feathery copse, nor stay
  Till thou hast skimmed o'er all the woodlands
    fair !
And when thou hast, then speeding back thy way,
  Tell me if she be there.

Sweet breeze ! that, wearied with the heat of noon,
  Upon a bank of daffodils didst die,
Oh, if thou lov'st me, quit thy perfumed swoon,
  And, all refreshed, hither and thither hie.
Traverse the glades where browse the dappled deer,
  Thrid the deep dells where none but thou mayst
    dare ;
And then, sweet breeze, returning to my ear,
  Whisper if she be there.

Sweet rivulet ! running far too fast to stay,
  Yet hear my plaint, e'en as thou rollest on !
I am alone—alone—both night and day,
  For she I love was with me, and is gone.

Oh, shouldst thou find her on the golden beach
  Whither thou speedest ocean's joys to share,
Remount thy course, despite what sophists teach,
  And tell me she is there.

Not there! nor there! not in the far-off sky,
  Close-keeping woods, or by the shining sea!
When lark, dove, breeze, and rivulet vainly try
  To find my sweet—oh, where then may she be?
Hath she then left me—me she vowed so dear,
  And she whose shadow dusks all other charms?
O foolish messengers! Look, look! She's here,
  Enfolded in my arms!

GRATA JUVENTAS.

ALFRED AUSTIN.

SHE trembles when I touch
  The tips of scarce-grown fingers,
Yet seems to think it overmuch
 If for a moment lingers
Grasp that I hardly meant for such.

She clutcheth toy or book,
  Or female hand beside her ;
Now with askant, unsettled look
  Inviteth, then doth hide her,
Like struggling lily in a brook.

Anon she darteth glance
  Athwart averted shoulder;
But when encouraged I advance
  A sudden waxing colder,
Her gaze lacks all significance.

Oh, were she younger still,
  Or more than a beginner,
I might control my troubled will,
  Or give it rein and win her:
But now she is nor good nor ill.

LADY MABEL.

ALFRED AUSTIN.

SIDE by side with Lady Mabel
   Sate I, with the sunshade down ;
In the distance hummed the Babel
   Of the many-footed town ;
There we sat with looks unstable,—
   Now of tenderness, of frown.

" Must we part ? or may I linger ?
   Wax the shadows, wanes the day."
Then, with voice of sweetest singer
   That hath all but died away,
" Go," she said ; but tightened finger
   Said articulately, " Stay !"

Face to face with Lady Mabel,
  With the gauzy curtains drawn,
Till a sense I am unable
  To portray, began to dawn ;
Till the slant sun flung the gable
  Far athwart the sleepy lawn.

" Now I go.   Adieu, adieu, love !
  This is weakness ; sweet, be strong.
Comes the footfall of the dew, love !
  Philomel's reminding song."
" Go," she said ; " but I go too, love
  Go with you— my life along !"

AT THE LATTICE.

ALFRED AUSTIN.

BEHIND the curtain,
  With glance uncertain,
    Peeps Pet Florence as I gaily ride ;
Half demurely,
But, though purely,
Most, most surely
Wishing she were riding, riding by my side.

In leafy alleys,
Where sunlight dallies,
Pleasant were it, bonnie, to be riding rein by rein ;
And where summer tosses,
All about in bosses,
Velvet verdant mosses,
Still more pleasant, surely, to dismount us and remain.

O thou Beauty!

Hanging ripe and fruity

At the muslined lattice in the drooping eve,

Whisper from the casement

If that blushing face meant,

"At the cottage basement,

Gallant, halt, I come to thee; I come to never leave."

But if those coy lashes

Stir for whoso dashes

Past the scented window in the fading light,

Close the lattice, sweetest;

Darkness were discreetest;

And, with bridle fleetest,

I will gallop onwards, unattended, through the night.

"FAULT-MENDING."

[*Extract.*]

Dr Barnard.

I LATELY thought no man alive
   Could e'er improve past forty-five,
     And ventured to assert it.
The observation was not new,
But seemed to me so just and true
     That none could controvert it.

"No, sir," said Johnson, "'tis not so ;
'Tis your mistake, and I can show
     An instance, if you doubt it.
You, who perhaps are forty-eight,
May still improve, 'tis not too late ;
     I wish you 'd set about it."

Encouraged thus to mend my faults,
I turned his counsel in my thoughts
　　Which way I could apply it;
Genius I knew was past my reach,
For who can learn what none can teach?
　　And wit—I could not buy it.

Then come, my friends, and try your skill;
You may improve me if you will,
　　(My books are at a distance :)
With you I 'll live and learn, and then
Instead of books I shall read men,
　　So lend me your assistance.

THE ARCHERY MEETING.

Thomas Haynes Bayly.

I.

THE archery meeting is fixed for the Third;
 The fuss that it causes is truly absurd;
 I 've bought summer bonnets for Rosa and
 Bess,
And now I must buy each an archery dress !
Without a green suit they would blush to be seen,
And poor little Rosa looks horrid in green.

II.

Poor fat little Rosa, she 's shooting all day !
She sends forth an arrow expertly, they say ;
But 'tis terrible when with exertion she warms,
And she seems to me getting such muscular arms ;

And if she should hit, 'twere as well if she missed,
Prize bracelets could never be placed on her wrists.

III.

Dear Bess, with her elegant figure and face,
Looks quite a Diana, the queen of the place;
But as for the shooting—she never takes aim;
She talks so and laughs so!—the *beaux* are to blame;
She doats on flirtation—but oh! by the bye,
'Twas awkward her shooting out Mrs Flint's eye!

IV.

They've made my poor husband an archer elect;
He dresses the part with prodigious effect;
A pair of nankeens, with a belt round his waist,
And a quiver of course, in which arrows are placed;
And a bow in his hand—oh! he looks of all things
Like a corpulent Cupid bereft of his wings!

V.

They dance on the lawn, and we mothers, alas!
Must sit on camp-stools with our feet in the grass;

My Flora and Bessy no partners attract !

The archery men are all *cross beaux* in fact !

Among the young ladies some hits there may be,

But still at my elbow two *misses* I see !

WON'T YOU?

Thomas Haynes Bayly.

I.

D O you remember when you heard

My lips breathe love's first faltering word?

You do, sweet—don't you?

When having wandered all the day,

Linked arm in arm, I dared to say,

"You 'll love me—won't you?"

II.

And when you blushed, and could not speak,

I fondly kissed your glowing cheek;

Did that affront you?

Oh, surely not; your eye exprest

No wrath—but said, perhaps in jest,

"You 'll love me—won't you?"

III.

I 'm sure my eyes replied, " I will ; "
And you believe that promise still ;
    You *do*, sweet—don't you?
Yes, yes ! when age has made our eyes
Unfit for questions or replies,
    You 'll love me—won't you?

DON'T TALK OF SEPTEMBER.

Thomas Haynes Bayly.

I.

DON'T talk of September!—a lady
  Must think it of all months the worst;
The men are preparing already
  To take themselves off on the First.
I try to arrange a small party,
  The girls dance together; how tame!
I 'd get up my game of écarté,
  But they go to bring down *their* game!

II.

Last month, their attention to quicken,
  A supper I knew was the thing;
But now from my turkey and chicken
  They 're tempted by birds on the wing!

They shoulder their terrible rifles,
(It's really too much for my nerves!)
And slighting my sweets and my trifles,
Prefer my Lord Harry's preserves!

III.

Miss Lovemore, with great consternation,
Now hears of the horrible plan,
And fears that her little flirtation
Was only a flash in the pan !
Oh ! marriage is hard of digestion,
The men are all sparing of words;
And now, 'stead of popping the question,
They set off to pop at the birds.

IV.

Go, false ones, your aim is so horrid,
That love at the sight of you dies ;
You care not for locks on the forehead,
The *locks* made by Manton you prize !
All thoughts sentimental exploding,
Like *flints* I behold you depart ;

You heed not, when priming and loading,
The load you have left on my heart !

v.

They talk about patent percussions,
And all preparations for sport ;
And those double-barrel discussions
Exhaust double bottles of port !
The dearest is deaf to my summons,
As off on his pony he jogs ;
A doleful condition is woman's ;
The men are all *gone to the dogs.*

YOU NEVER KNEW ANNETTE.

Thomas Haynes Bayly.

I.

YOU praise each youthful form you see,
　　And love is still your theme ;
　　And when you win no praise from me
　　You say how cold I seem.
　　You know not what it is to pine
　　　With ceaseless vain regret ;
　　You never felt a love like mine,—
　　　You never knew Annette.

II.

For ever changing, still you rove,
　　As I in boyhood roved ;
But when you tell me this is love,
　　It proves you never loved,

To many idols you have knelt,
  And therefore soon forget;
But what I feel you never felt,—
  You never knew Annette.

KIRTLE RED.

W. H. Bellamy.

DAMSEL fair, on a summer's day—
  —Sing heigh, sing ho, for the summer!
Sat under a tree in a kirtle gray,
Singing, "Somebody's late at tryst to-day;
Gather ye rosebuds while ye may,
  Or the leaves may fall in summer!"

Answered a little bird overhead—
  As birds will do in summer;
"Somebody *has* kept tryst," it said,
"With somebody else in a kirtle red,
And they are going to be married."
  —Sing heigh, sing ho, for the summer!

"With all my heart, little bird," said she ;

   —Sing heigh, sing ho, for the summer

"He's welcome to kirtle red for me ;

Somebody's fast, while somebody's free !

There's nothing, no, nothing, like libertie !"

   —Sing heigh, sing ho, for the summer ! *

* Reprinted, from the song of "Kirtle Red," by permission of Messrs Boosey & Co.

TO AN UTTER STRANGER.

E. F. BLANCHARD.

IT cannot be said I 've no love
  Because I 've no sighs ;
  Believe me not utterly blind,
  For slighting your eyes.
No violet,—purple, not red,—
  Can rival their hue ;
Maria's are hazel you know—
  Well, hazel will do.
I will not deny that your hair
  Is black as the wings

Of ravens—I'm tired of ravens—
  The troublesome things.
Maria's is certainly auburn,
  Whatever you say—
Rich colour that runs little risk
  Of changing to gray.
And though it appears that her lips
  Are not " stung by bees,"
The kisses they'll possibly give
  Will equally please.
I cannot pretend to assert
  Her teeth to be pearls—
Her locks to be hyacinth leaves—
  They're curls—simply curls.
And down where they nestle below
  Her unswanlike neck,
A bosom that's not alabaster
  They happily deck.
The light heart that's dancing beneath
  That breast, gives me life ;
The lips utter merely one word—
  Sweet sentiment—wife.

It cannot be said I 've no heart
Because it won't break—
Life or soul, because I decline
To die for your sake.

THE PET CANARY.

E. LAMAN BLANCHARD.

BIRD of the household! songster of home,
    Whose notes in a wild burst of harmony
      come,
Like a voice from the woods, or a song by the stream
Of Youth's early May-time and Love's early dream;
Thy cage is no prison, no captive thus sings,
And free in the sun flies the gold of thy wings.
"Pretty Dick!" let thy mistress, sweet, whisper a
    word—
Her heart is a captive much more than her bird.

Oh, would thou couldst utter her thoughts in thy lay,
Then free shouldst thou fly to the one far away,

D

And tell him how oft with her bird in the cage

She has talked of the absent and looked at his gage.

Thou shouldst give him the kiss I am giving to thee,

And say it was sent as a token from me.

" Pretty Dick ! " if he told you no more we should part,

Thy wings could not flutter much more than my heart.

THE TREATY.

Caroline Bowles.

NEVER tell me of loving by measure and weight,
  As one's merits may lack or abound;
  As if love could be carried to market like
    skate,
And cheapened for so much a pound.

If it can—if *yours* can, let them have it who care—
  You and I, friend! shall never agree—
Pack up and to market be off with your ware;
  It's a great deal too common for me.

D' ye linger?—d' ye laugh?—I 'm in earnest, I vow—.
  Though perhaps over-hasty a thought;
If you 're thinking to close with my terms as they are,
  Well and good—but I won't bate a jot.

You must love me—we 'll note the chief articles now,
  To preclude all mistakes in our pact—
And I 'll pledge you, unasked and beforehand, my vow,
  To give double for all I exact.

You must love me—not only through " evil report,"
  When its falsehood you more than divine;
But when upon earth I can only resort
  To your heart as a voucher for mine.

You must love—*not my faults*—but in *spite* of them—
    me,
  For the very caprices that vex you:
Nay, the more, should you chance (as it 's likely) to see
  'Tis my special delight to perplex you.

You must love me, albeit the world I offend
  By impertinence, whimsies, conceit ;
While assured (if you are not, all treaty must end)
  That I never can stoop to deceit.

While assured (as you must be, or there too we part)
  That were all the world leagued against you,
To loosen one hair of your hold on my heart
  Would be more than " life's labours " could do.

You must love me, howe'er I may take things amiss,
  Whereof you in all conscience stand clear ;
And although, when you 'd fain make it up with a
      kiss,
  Your reward be a box on the ear.

You must love me—not only when smiling and gay,
  Complying, sweet tempered, and civil ;
But when moping, and frowning, and forward—or say
  The thing plain out—as cross as the devil.

You must love me in all moods—in seriousness, sport;
     Under all change of circumstance too :
Apart, or together, in crowds, or—in short,
     You must love me—*because I love you.*

WHAT THE WOLF REALLY SAID TO LITTLE RED RIDING-HOOD.

BRET HARTE.

WONDERING maiden, so puzzled and fair,
   Why dost thou murmur and ponder and
      stare?
" Why are my eyelids so open and wild? "
Only the better to see with, my child !
Only the better and clearer to view
Cheeks that are rosy, and eyes that are blue.

Dost thou still wonder, and ask why these arms
Fill thy soft bosom with tender alarms,
Swaying so wickedly ?—are they misplaced
Clasping or shielding some delicate waist?

Hands whose coarse sinews may fill you with fear
Only the better protect you, my dear!

Little Red Riding-Hood, when in the street,
Why do I press your small hand when we meet?
Why, when you timidly offered your cheek,
Why did I sigh, and why didn't I speak?
Why, well: you see—if the truth must appear—
I'm not your grandmother, Riding-Hood, dear!

NEIGHBOUR NELLY.

Robert B. Brough.

I'M in love with neighbour Nelly,
   Though I know she's only ten,
   While, alas! I'm eight-and-forty—
And the *marriedst* of men!
I've a wife who weighs me double,
   I've three daughters all with *beaux* :
I've a son with noble whiskers,
   Who at me turns up his nose.

Though a square-toes, and a fogey,
   Still I've sunshine in my heart :
Still I'm fond of cakes and marbles,
   Can appreciate a tart.

I can love my neighbour Nelly
  Just as though I were a boy :
I could hand her nuts and apples
  From my depths of corduroy.

She is tall, and growing taller,
  She is vigorous of limb :
(You should see her play at cricket
  With her little brother Jim.)
She has eyes as blue as damsons,
  She has pounds of auburn curls ;
She regrets the game of leapfrog
  Is prohibited to girls.

I adore my neighbour Nelly,
  I invite her in to tea :
And I let her nurse the baby—
  All her pretty ways to see.
Such a darling bud of woman,
  Yet remote from any teens,—

I have learnt from neighbour Nelly
    What the girl's doll-instinct means.

Oh, to see her with the baby!
    He adores her more than I,—
How she choruses his crowing,—
    How she hushes every cry!
How she loves to pit his dimples
    With her light forefinger deep,
How she boasts to me in triumph
    When she's got him off to sleep!

We must part, my neighbour Nelly,
    For the summers quickly flee;
And your middle-aged admirer
    Must supplanted quickly be.
Yet as jealous as a mother,—
    A distempered cankered churl,
I look vainly for the setting
    To be worthy such a pearl.

A LIKENESS.

[*Extract.*]

ROBERT BROWNING.

SOME people hang portraits up
In a room where they dine or sup,
And the wife clinks tea-things under ;
And her cousin, he stirs his cup,
Asks, " Who was the lady, I wonder ? "
" 'Tis a daub John bought at a sale,"
Quoth the wife,—looks black as thunder :
" What a shade beneath her nose !
Snuff-taking I suppose,"
Adds the cousin, while John's corns ail.

Or else, there 's no wife in the case,

But the portrait 's queen of the place,

Alone 'mid the spoils

Of youth,—masks, gloves, and foils,

And pipe-sticks, rose, cherry-tree, jasmine,

And the long whip, the tandem-lasher,

And the cast from a fist—("Not, alas! mine,

But my master's, the Tipton Slasher,")

And the cards where pistol-balls mark ace,

And a satin shoe used for cigar-case,

And the chamois-horns—("Shot in the Chablais,")

And prints,—Rarey drumming on Cruiser,

And Sayers, our champion, the bruiser,

And the little edition of Rabelais:

Where a friend, with both hands in his pockets,

May saunter up close to examine it,

And remark a good deal of Jane Lamb in it,

But the eyes are half out of their sockets;

That hair 's not so bad where the gloss is,

But they 've made the girl's nose a proboscis:

Jane Lamb that we danced with at Vichy.

What! is she not Jane? then, who is she?

All that I own is a print,
An etching, a mezzotint ;
'Tis a study, a fancy, a fiction,
Yet a fact (take my conviction,
Because it has more than a hint
Of a certain face I never
Saw elsewhere touch or trace of,
In women I 've seen the face of)—
Just an etching, and, so far, clever.

S O N G.

Robert Browning.

I.

NAY, but you, who do not love her,
   Is she not pure gold, my mistress?
   Holds earth aught—speak truth—above her?
  Aught like this tress, see, and this tress,
And this last fairest tress of all,
So fair, see, ere I let it fall!

II.

Because, you spend your lives in praising;
   To praise, you search the wide world over;
So, why not witness, calmly gazing,
   If earth holds aught—speak truth—above her?
Above this tress, and this I touch
But cannot praise, I love so much!

YOUTH AND ART.

[*Extract.*]

ROBERT BROWNING.

IT once might have been, once only :
  We lodged in a street together,
  You, a sparrow on the housetop lonely,
I, a lone she-bird of his feather.

Your trade was with sticks and clay ;
  You thumbed, thrust, patted and polished,
Then laughed, "They will see some day
  Smith made, and Gibson demolished !"

My business was song, song, song ;
  I chirped, cheeped, trilled, and twittered,
"Kate Brown's on the boards ere long,
  And Grisi's existence embittered !"

I earned no more by a warble
   Than you by a sketch in plaster;
You wanted a piece of marble,
   I needed a music-master.

.   .   .   .   .

Why did not you pinch a flower
   In a pellet of clay, and fling it?
Why did not I put a power
   Of thanks in a look, or sing it?

No, no! you would not be rash,
   Nor I rasher and something over:
You 've to settle yet Gibson's hash,
   And Grisi yet lives in clover.

Each life 's unfulfilled, you see;
   It hangs still, patchy and scrappy:
We have not sighed deep, laughed free,
   Starved, feasted, despaired,—been happy.

E

. . . . .

And nobody calls you a dunce,

And people suppose me clever:

This could but have happened once,

And we missed it, lost it for ever.

AMY'S CRUELTY.

MRS BROWNING.

FAIR Amy of the terraced house !
    Assist me to discover
Why you, who would not hurt a mouse,
    Can torture so a lover?

You give your coffee to the cat,
    You stroke the dog for coming,
And all your face grows kinder at
    The little brown bee's humming.

But when *he* haunts your door—the town
    Marks coming and marks going—
You seem to have stitched your eyelids down
    To that long piece of sewing !

You never give a look, not you,
  Nor drop him a " Good-morning,"
To keep his long day warm and blue,
  So fretted by your scorning.

She shook her head—" The mouse and bee
  For crumb or flower will linger ;
The dog is happy at my knee,
  The cat purrs at my finger.

" But *he*—to *him*, the least thing given
  Means great things at a distance :
He wants my world, my sun, my heaven,
  Soul, body, whole existence.

" They say love gives as well as takes ;
  But I 'm a simple maiden,—
My mother's first smile when she wakes
  I still have smiled and prayed in.

" I only know my mother's love,
  Which gives all and asks nothing ;

And this new loving sets the groove
  Too much the way of loathing.

" Unless he gives me all in 'change,
    I forfeit all things by him ;
The risk is terrible and strange ;
    I tremble, doubt—deny him.

" His sweetest friend, or hardest foe,
    Best angel, or worst devil,
I either hate—or love him so,
    I can't be merely civil !

" Such love 's a cowslip-ball to fling,
    A moment's pretty pastime ;
I give—all me, if anything,
    The first time, and the last time.

" Dear neighbour of the trellised house !
    A man should murmur never,
Though treated worse than dog or mouse,
    Till doated on for ever."

A FALSE STEP.

MRS BROWNING.

WEET, thou hast trod on a heart.
 Pass! there's a world full of men,
And women as fair as thou art
 Must do such things now and then.

Thou only hast stepped unaware,—
 Malice, not one can impute;
And why should a heart have been there
 In the way of a fair woman's foot?

It was not a stone that could trip,
 Nor was it a thorn that could rend:
Put up thy proud underlip!
 'Twas merely the heart of a friend.

And yet peradventure one day,
   Thou, sitting alone at the glass,
Remarking the bloom gone away,
   Where the smile in its dimplement was,

And seeking around thee in vain
   From hundreds who flattered before
Such a word as, " Oh, not in the main
   Do I hold thee less precious, but more !"

Thou 'lt sigh, very like, on thy part,
   "Of all I have known or can know,
I wish I had only that heart
   I trod upon ages ago !"

A MAN'S REQUIREMENTS.

Mrs Browning.

LOVE me, sweet, with all thou art,
 Feeling, thinking, seeing ;
Love me in the lightest part,
 Love me in full being.

Love me with thine open youth
 In its frank surrender ;
With the vowing of thy mouth,
 With its silence tender.

Love me with thine azure eyes,
 Made for earnest granting ;
Taking colour from the skies,
 Can Heaven's truth be wanting ?

Love me with their lids that fall
  Snow-like at first meeting;
Love me with thine heart, that all
  Neighbours then see beating.

Love me with thine hand stretched out
  Freely—open-minded:
Love me with thy loitering foot—
  Hearing one behind it.

Love me with thy voice, that turns
  Sudden faint above me;
Love me with thy blush that burns
  When I murmur, *Love me!*

Love me with thy thinking soul
  Break it to love-sighing;
Love me with thy thoughts that roll
  On through living—dying.

Love me in thy gorgeous airs,
  When the world has crowned thee;

Love me kneeling at thy prayers,
  With the angels round thee.

Love me pure, as musers do,
  Up the woodlands shady;
Love me gaily, fast and true,
  As a winsome lady.

Through all hopes that keep us brave,
  Further off or nigher;
Love me for the house and grave,
  And for something higher.

Thus, if thou wilt prove me, dear,
  Woman's love no fable,
I will love *thee*—half a year—
  As a man is able.

O N   F A M E.

Lord Byron.

OH, talk not to me of a name great in story;
The days of our youth are the days of our
glory;
And the myrtle and ivy of sweet two-and-twenty
Are worth all your laurels, though ever so plenty.

What are garlands and crowns to the brow that is
wrinkled?
'Tis but as a dead flower with May-dew besprinkled:
Then away with all such from the head that is hoary!
What care I for the wreaths that can *only* give glory?

O Fame! if I e'er took delight in thy praises,
'Twas less for the sake of thy high-sounding phrases,

Than to see the bright eyes of the dear one discover
She thought that I was not unworthy to love her.

There chiefly I sought thee—*there* only I found thee ;
Her glance was the best of the rays that surround
    thee :
When its spark led o'er aught that was bright in my
    story,
I knew it was love, and I felt it was glory.

ODE TO TOBACCO.

C. S. C.

THOU who, when fears attack,
  Bidd'st them avaunt, and black
  Care, at the horseman's back
    Perching, unseatest;
Sweet when the morn is grey;
Sweet when they 've cleared away
Lunch; and at close of day
    Possibly sweetest:

I have a liking old
For thee, though manifold
Stories, I know, are told
    Not to thy credit;

How one (or two at most)
Drops make a cat a ghost—
Useless, except to roast—
        Doctors have said it.

How they who use fuzees
All grow by slow degrees
Brainless as chimpanzees,
        Meagre as lizards;
Go mad, and beat their wives;
Plunge (after shocking lives)
Razors and carving-knives
        Into their gizzards.

Confound such knavish tricks!
Yet I know five or six
Smokers, who freely mix
        Still with their neighbours;
Jones (who, I 'm glad to say,
Asked leave of Mrs J.)
Daily absorbs a clay
        After his labours.

Cats may have had their goose
Cooked by tobacco-juice;
Still why deny its use
　　Thoughtfully taken?
We 're not as tabbies are:
Smith, take a fresh cigar!
Jones, the tobacco-jar!
　　Here 's to thee, Bacon!

SORACTE.

[Extract from translation by C. S. C.]

HORACE.

ASK not what future suns shall bring,
   Count to-day gain, whate'er it chance
     To be ; nor, young man, scorn the dance,
Nor deem sweet love an idle thing,

Ere Time thy April youth hath changed
   To sourness.   Park and public walk
     Attract thee now, and whispered talk
At twilight meetings pre-arranged;

Hear now the pretty laugh that tells
   In what dim corner lurks thy love;
     And snatch a bracelet or a glove
From wrist or hand that scarce rebels.

LINES

SUGGESTED BY THE FOURTEENTH OF FEBRUARY.

[*Extract.*]

C. S. C.

ERE the morn the east has crimsoned,
  When the stars are twinkling there
(As they did in Watt's Hymns, and
  Made him wonder what they were),
When the forest nymphs are beading
  Fern and flower with silvery dew—
My infallible proceeding
  Is to wake and think of you.

When the hunter's ringing bugle
  Sounds farewell to field and copse,
And I sit before my frugal
  Meal of gravy-soup and chops;

When (as Gray remarks) " the moping
   Owl doth to the moon complain,"
And the hour suggests eloping—
   Fly my thoughts to you again.

.   .   .   .   .

Give me hope, the least, the dimmest,
   Ere I drain the poisoned cup ;
Tell me I may tell the chymist
   Not to make that arsenic up !
Else, this heart shall soon cease throbbing ;
   And when, musing o'er my bones,
Travellers ask, " Who killed Cock Robin ? "
   They 'll be told, " Miss Sarah J——s."

IN THE GLOAMING.

C. S. C.

ON the gloaming to be roaming, where the crested waves are foaming,
  And the sly mermaidens combing locks that ripple to their feet;
What the gloaming is, I never made the ghost of an endeavour
                                        [be sweet.
  To discover—but whatever were the hour, it would

"To their feet," I say; for Leech's sketch indisputably teaches
                                        [ugly tails,
  That the mermaids of our beaches do not end in
Nor have homes among the corals; but are shod with neat balmorals,
  An arrangement no one quarrels with, as many might with scales.

Sweet to roam beneath a shady cliff of course with
    some young lady,
  Lalage, Neæra, Haidee, or Elaine, or Mary Ann :
Love, you dear delusive dream you ! very sweet your
    victims deem you,
  When, heard only by the seamew, they talk all the
    stuff they can.

Sweet to haste, a licensed lover, to Miss Pinkerton
    the glover,
  Having managed to discover what is dear Neæra's
    size ;
P'raps to touch that wrist so slender, as your tiny
    gift you tender,
  And to read you 're no offender in those laughing
    hazel eyes.

Then to hear her call you " Harry," when she makes
    you fetch and carry,
  O young man about to marry ! what a blessed thing
    it is !

To be photographed together—cased in pretty
    Russia leather—
  Hear her gravely doubting whether they have spoilt
    your honest phiz!

Then to bring your plighted fair one first a ring—a
    rich and rare one—
  Next a bracelet, if she 'll wear one, and a heap of
    things beside ;
And serenely bending o'er her, to inquire if it would
    bore her
  To say when her own adorer may aspire to call her
    bride ?

Then, the days of courtship over, with your wife to
    start for Dover
  Or Dieppe—and live in clover evermore, whate'er
    befalls :
For I 've read in many a novel that, unless they 've
    souls that grovel,
  Folks *prefer*, in fact, a hovel to your dreary marble
    halls.

C. S. C.

"UNDER the trees!" who but agrees
    That there is magic in words such as these?
    Promptly one sees shake in the breeze
Stately lime avenues haunted of bees :
Where, looking far over buttercupped leas,
Lads and " fair shes " (that is Byron's, and he 's
An authority) lie very much at their ease ;
Taking their teas, or their duck and green peas,
Or, if they prefer it, their plain bread and cheese :
Not objecting at all, though its rather a squeeze,
And the glass is, I daresay, at eighty degrees.
Some get up glees, and are mad about Ries,
And Sainton, and Tamberlik's thrilling high C's ;

Or, if painter, hold forth upon Hunt and Maclise,

And the breadth of that landscape of Lee's;

Or, if learned, on nodes and the moon's apogees,

Or, if serious, on something of A. K. H. B.'s,

Or the latest attempt to convert the Chaldees;

Or, in short, about all things, from earthquakes to
    fleas.

Some sit in twos or (less frequently) threes,

With their innocent lambswool or book on their
    knees,

And talk and enact any nonsense you please,

As they gaze into eyes that are blue as the seas;

And you hear an occasional, " Harry, don't tease,"

From the sweetest of lips in the softest of keys,

And other remarks, which to me are Chinese.

And fast the time flees, till a lady-like sneeze,

Or a portly papa's more elaborate wheeze,

Makes Miss Tabitha seize on her brown muffatees,

And announce as a fact that it's going to freeze,

And that young people ought to attend to their P's

And their Q's, and not court every form of disease;

Then Tommy eats up the three last ratifias,

And pretty Louise wraps her *robe de cerise*

Round a bosom as tender as Widow Machree's,

And (in spite of the pleas of her lorn *vis-à-vis*)

Goes and wraps up her uncle—a patient of Skey's,

Who is prone to catch chills, like all old Bengalese :—

But at bedtime I trust he'll remember to grease

The bridge of his nose, and preserve his rupees

From the premature clutch of his fond legatees;

Or at least have no fees to pay any M.D.'s

For the cold his niece caught sitting under the trees.

THE ROMANCE OF A GLOVE.

H. SAVILLE CLARKE.

ERE on my desk it lies,
 Here as the daylight dies,
 One small glove just her size—
  Six and a quarter;
 Pearl-gray, a colour neat,
 Deux boutons all complete,
 Faint-scented, soft and sweet;
  Could glove be smarter?

 Can I the day forget,
 Years ago, when the pet
 Gave it me?—where we met
  Still I remember;

Then 'twas the summer-time ;
Now as I write this rhyme
Children love pantomime—
   'Tis in December.

Fancy my boyish bliss
Then when she gave me this,
And how the frequent kiss
   Crumpled its fingers ;
Then she was fair and kind,
Now, when I 've changed my mind,
Still some scent undefined
   On the glove lingers.

Though she 's a matron sage,
Yet I have kept the gage ;
While, as I pen this page,
   Still comes a goddess,
Her eldest daughter, fair,
With the same eyes and hair :
Happy the arm, I swear,
   That clasps her boddice.

Heaven grant her fate be bright,
And her step ever light
As it will be to-night,
   First in the dances.
Why did her mother prove
False when I dared to love ?
Zounds ! I shall burn the glove !
   This my romance is.

KENSINGTON.

ARTHUR H. CLOUGH.

ON grass, on gravel, in the sun,
　　Or now beneath the shade,
They went, in pleasant Kensington,
　　A prentice and a maid.
That Sunday morning's April glow,
　　How should it not impart
A stir about the veins that flow
　　To feed the youthful heart?
Ah! years may come, and years may bring
　　The truth that is not bliss,
But will they bring another thing
　　That can compare with this?

I read it in that arm she lays
　　So soft on his; her mien,

Her step, her very gown betrays
  (What in her eyes were seen)
That not in vain the young buds round,
  The cawing birds above,
The air, the incense of the ground,
  Are whispering, breathing love.

Oh, odours of new-budding rose,
  Oh, lily's chaste perfume,
Oh, fragrance that didst first unclose
  The young creation's bloom !
Ye hang around me, while in sun
  Anon, and now in shade,
I watched in pleasant Kensington
  The prentice and the maid.
Ah! years may come, and years may bring
  The truth that is not bliss,
But will they bring another thing
  That will compare with this ?

GOING WITH THE STREAM.

[*Extract.*]

ARTHUR H. CLOUGH.

UPON the water in a boat
   I sit and sketch, as there we float,
   The scene is fair, the stream is strong,
I sketch it as we float along.

The stream is strong, and as I sit
And view the picture that we quit,
It flows, and flows, and bears the boat,
And I sit sketching as we float.

Still as we go, the things I see,
E'en as I see them, cease to be,
The angles shift, and with the boat
The whole perspective seems to float.

Yet still I look, and still I sit

Adjusting, shaping, altering it ;

And still the current bears the boat,

And me, still sketching as I float.

THE EXCHANGE.

Samuel T. Coleridge.

WE pledged our hearts, my love and I,—
　　I in my arms the maiden clasping:
　　I could not tell the reason why,
But oh! I trembled like an aspen.

Her father's love she bade me gain;
　　I went, and shook like any reed!
I strove to act the man—in vain!
　　We had exchanged our hearts indeed.

A SUMMER SONG.

MORTIMER COLLINS.

UMMER is sweet, ay! summer is sweet,—
 Minna mine with the brown, brown eyes:
 Red are the roses under his feet,
 Clear the blue of his windless skies.
Pleasant it is in a boat to glide
 On a river whose ripples to ocean haste,
With indolent fingers fretting the tide,
 And an indolent arm round a darling waist—
And to see, as the western purple dies,
Hesper mirrored in brown, brown eyes.

Summer is fleet, ah! summer is fleet,—
 Minna mine with the brown, brown eyes:

G

Onward travel his flying feet,

    And the mystical colours of autumn rise.

Clouds will gather round evening star—

    Sorrow may silence our first gay rhyme,—

The river's swift ripples flow tardier far

    Than the golden minutes of love's sweet time :

But to me, whom omnipotent love makes wise,

There's endless summer in brown, brown eyes.

MY OLD COAT.

MORTIMER COLLINS.

I.

THIS old velvet coat has grown queer, I admit,
  And changed is the colour and loose is the fit ;
  Though to beauty it certainly cannot aspire,
'Tis a cozy old coat for a seat by the fire.

II.

When I first put it on, it was awfully swell;
I went to a picnic, met Lucy Lepel,
Made a hole in the heart of that sweet little girl,
And disjointed the nose of her lover, the earl.

III.

We rambled away o'er the moorland together ;
My coat was bright purple, and so was the heather,
And so was the sunset that blazed in the west,
As Lucy's fair tresses were laid on my breast.

IV.

We plighted our troth 'neath that sunset aflame,
But Lucy returned to her earl all the same ;   .
She's a grandmamma now, and is going down-hill,
But my old velvet coat is a friend to me still.

V.

It was built by a tailor of mighty renown,
Whose art is no longer the talk of the town :
A magical picture my memory weaves
When I thrust my tired arms through its easy old
    sleeves.

VI.

I see in my fire, through the smoke of my pipe,
Sweet maidens of old that are long over-ripe,
And a troop of old cronies, right gay cavaliers,
Whose guineas paid well for champagne at Watier's.

VII.

A strong generation, who drank, fought, and kissed,
Whose hands never trembled, whose shots never missed,
Who lived a quick life, for their pulses beat high—
We remember them well, sir, my old coat and I.

VIII.

Ah, gone is the age of wild doings at court,

Rotten boroughs, knee-breeches, hair-triggers, and
    port;

Still I 've got a magnum to moisten my throat,

And I 'll drink to the past in my tattered old coat.

THE BEST THING SAID TO-NIGHT.

Mortimer Collins.

AROUND the fire, past midnight, when the girls
  Were sleeping, let us hope, their beauty-sleep
  In nests of delicate fragrance, there remained
Just two or three to smoke that last cigar
And taste the sweet o' the night.   Quoth one of us,
Knocking the white ash indolently off,
Lest it should fall upon his lounging coat
Like sudden snow upon a purple moor,
"*What was the best thing said to-night?*"   A flow
Of talk succeeded : one man's epigram,
Another's pretty speech to Isabel,
The wild young poet's lyric oratory
Half-way 'twixt the Agora and Colney Hatch,
The impromptu in the style of *Vivian Grey*

About *Disraeli*—these and fifty more
The men discussed until discussion yawned
And the last seltzer quenched the last cigar,
And everybody went to bed.   But I,
I knew full well the best thing said that night,
When she who wore the buds of cyclamen
Stood in the odorous twilight 'mid the flowers,
While a caressing spray of some white bloom
Over her rose-flushed shoulder fell.   I knew,
And wrote it down on a Vitellian* leaf—
A little tablet for love's lusive rhyme.
Who will, may read.

I.

O darling eyelids' delicate droop !
 O little sweet mouth, so red, so pure !
There in the twilight while I stoop,
 Beautiful Amoret looks demure.
There 's a word to whisper : who can guess ?
Will it be *No*, sweet ? will it be *Yes ?*

* " Non dum legerit hos licet puella,
 Novit quid cupiant Vitelliani."

II.

Listen the flowers that word to learn
　　Which the little sweet mouth must say to me ;
Faintly it flutters the fairy fern :
　　What will it be ? O what will it be ?
Tender the gleam in those eyes of light
As she says *the best thing said to-night.*

A GAME OF CHESS.

MORTIMER COLLINS.

I.

TERRACE and lawn are white with frost,
  Whose fretwork flowers upon the panes—
A mocking dream of summer, lost
  'Mid winter's icy chains.

II.

White-hot, indoors, the great logs gleam,
  Veiled by a flickering flame of blue :
I see my love as in a dream—
  Her eyes are azure, too.

III.

She binds her hair behind her ears
  (Each little ear so like a shell),
Touches her ivory Queen, and fears
  She is not playing well.

IV.

For me, I think of nothing less :
  I think how those pure pearls become her—
And which is sweetest, winter chess
        Or garden strolls in summer.

V.

O linger, frost, upon the pane !
  O faint blue flame, still softly rise !
O dear one, thus with me remain,
        That I may watch thine eyes !

AD CHLOEN, M.A.,

Fresh from her Cambridge Examination.

MORTIMER COLLINS.

LADY, very fair are you,
    And your eyes are very blue,—
        —And your hose ;—
And your brow is like the snow,
And the various things you know
        Goodness knows.

And the rose-flush on your cheek,
And your Algebra and Greek
        Perfect are ;
And that loving lustrous eye
Recognises in the sky
        Every star.

You have pouting piquant lips,
You can doubtless an eclipse
        Calculate ;
But for your cerulean hue
I had certainly from you
        Met my fate.

If by an arrangement dual
I were Adams mixed with Whewell,
        Then some day
I, as wooer, perhaps might come
To so sweet an Artium
        Magistra.

CHLOE, M.A.,

Ad amantem suum.

Mortimer Collins.

CARELESS rhymer! it is true
That my favourite colour's blue:
   But am I
To be made a victim, sir,
If to puddings I prefer
   Cambridge π?

If with giddier girls I play
Croquet through the summer day
   On the turf,
Then at night ('tis no great boon)
Let me study how the moon
   Sways the surf.

Tennyson's idyllic verse
Surely suits me none the worse
     If I seek
Old Sicilian birds and bees—
Music of sweet Sophocles—
     Golden Greek.

You have said my eyes are blue ;
There may be a fairer hue,
     Perhaps,—and yet
It is surely not a sin
If I keep my secrets in
     Violet.

MY OLD ARM-CHAIR.

[*Extract.*]

Barry Cornwall.

LET poets coin their golden dreams ;
Let lovers weave their vernal themes ;
And paint the earth all fair.
To me no such bright fancies throng :
I sing a humble hearthstone song,
Of thee,—my old arm-chair !

Poor—faded—ragged—crazy—old,—
Thou 'rt yet worth thrice thy weight in gold ;
Ay ! though thy back be bare :
For thou hast held a world of worth,
A load of heavenly human earth,—
My old arm-chair !

Here sate—ah ! many a year ago,
When, young, I nothing cared to know
   Of life or its great aim,—
Friends (gentle hearts) who smiled and shed
Brief sunshine on my boyish head :
   At last the wild clouds came,—

And vain desires, and hopes dismayed,
And fears that cast the earth in shade,
   My heart did fret ;
And dreaming wonders, foul and fair ;
And who then filled mine ancient chair,
   I now forget.

Then Love came—Love !—without his wings,
Low murmuring here a thousand things
   Of one I once thought fair ;
'Twas here he laughed, and bound my eyes,
Taking me, boy, by sweet surprise,
   Here,—in my own arm-chair.

How I escaped from that soft pain,
And (nothing lessoned) fell again
   Into another snare,
And how again Fate set me free,
Are secrets 'tween my soul and me,—
   Me, and my old arm-chair.

Years fade :—Old Time doth all he can :
The soft youth hardens into man;
   The vapour Fame
Dissolves : Care's scars indent our brow—
Friends fail us in our need :—but thou
   Art still the same.

THE WINTER NOSEGAY.

WILLIAM COWPER.

HAT Nature, alas! has denied
    To the delicate growth of our isle,
Art has in a measure supplied,
    And winter is decked with a smile.
See, Mary, what beauties I bring
    From the shelter of that sunny shed,
Where the flowers have the charms of the spring,
    Though abroad they are frozen and dead.

'Tis a bower of Arcadian sweets,
    Where Flora is still in her prime,
A fortress to which she retreats
    From the cruel assaults of the clime.

While earth wears a mantle of snow,
　These pinks are as fresh and as gay
As the fairest and sweetest that blow
　On the beautiful bosom of May.

See how they have safely survived
　The frowns of a sky so severe ;
Such Mary's true love, that has lived
　Through many a turbulent year.
The charms of the late-blowing rose,
　Seem graced with a livelier hue,
And the winter of sorrow best shows
　The truth of a friend such as you.

THE SYMPTOMS OF LOVE.

WILLIAM COWPER.

WOULD my Delia know if I love? let her take
My last thought at night, and the first when
    I wake;
When my prayers and best wishes preferred for her
    sake.

Let her guess what I muse on when, rambling alone,
I stride o'er the stubble each day with my gun,
Never ready to shoot till the covey is flown.

Let her think what odd whimsies I have in my brain,
When I read one page over and over again,
And discover at last that I read it in vain.

Let her say why so fixed and so steady my look,
Without ever regarding the person who spoke,
Still affecting to laugh without hearing the joke.

Or why when with pleasure her praises I hear
(That sweetest of melody sure to my ear),
I attend and at once inattentive appear.

And lastly, when summoned to drink to my flame,
Let her guess why I never once mention her name,
Though herself and the woman I love are the same.

WITH A PURSE.

WILLIAM COWPER.

MY gentle Anne, whom heretofore,
　　When I was young, and thou no more
　　Than plaything for a nurse,
I danced and fondled on my knee,
A kitten both in size and glee,
　　I thank thee for my purse.

Gold pays the worth of all things here ;
But not of love ;—that gem's too dear
　　For richest rogues to win it ;
I therefore, as a proof of love,
Esteem thy present far above
　　The best things kept within it.

A VICE

Austin Dobson.

THOUGH the voice of modern schools
      Has demurred,
By the dreamy Asian creed
      'Tis averred,
That the souls of men, released
From their bodies when deceased,
Sometimes enter in a beast,—
      Or a bird.

I have watched you long, Avice,—
      Watched you so,
I have found your secret out ;
      And I know

That the restless ribboned things,
　Where your slope of shoulder springs,
Are but undeveloped wings,
　　　　　　That will grow.

When you enter in a room,
　　　　　　It is stirred
With the wayward, flashing flight
　　　　　　Of a bird;
And you speak—and bring with you
Leaf and sun-ray, bud and blue,
And the wind-breath and the dew,
　　　　　　At a word.

When you called to me my name,
　　　　　　Then again
When I heard your single cry
　　　　　　In the lane,
All the sound was as the " sweet "
Which the birds to birds repeat
In their thank-song to the heat
　　　　　　After rain.

When you sang the *Schwalbenlied*,—

              'Twas absurd,—

But it seemed no human note

              That I heard ;

For your strain had all the trills,

All the little shakes and stills,

Of the over-song that rills

              From a bird.

You have just their eager, quick

              Airs de tête,

All their flush and fever-heat

              When elate ;

Every birdlike nod and beck,

And a bird's own curve of neck

When she gives a little peck

              To her mate.

When you left me, only now,

              In that furred,

Puffed, and feathered Polish dress,

              I was spurred

Just to catch you, O my sweet,
By the bodice trim and neat,—
Just to feel your heart a-beat,
                    Like a bird.

Yet alas! Love's light you deign
                    But to wear
As the dew upon your plumes,
                    And you care
Not a whit for rest or hush;
But the leaves, the lyric gush,
And the wing-power, and the rush
                    Of the air.

So I dare not woo you, sweet,
                    For a day,
Lest I lose you in a flash,
                    As I may;
Did I tell you tender things,
You would shake your sudden wings;—
You would start from him who sings,
                    And away.

POT-POURRI.

Austin Dobson.

" Si jeunesse savait ! "

PLUNGE my hand among the leaves :—
  An alien touch but dust perceives,
    Nought else supposes ;—
For me those fragrant ruins raise
Clear memory of the vanished days
    When they were roses.

" If youth but knew !" Ah, "if," in truth !—
I can recall with what gay youth,
    To what light chorus,
Unsobered yet by time or change,
We roamed the many-gabled Grange,
    All life before us :

Braved the old clock-tower's dust and damp
To catch the dim Arthurian camp
　　In misty distance ;
Peered at the still-room's sacred stores,
And rapped at walls for sliding doors
　　Of feigned existence.

What need had we for thoughts or cares?
The hot sun parched the old parterres
　　And dahlia closes :
We roused the rooks with rounds and glees,
Played hide-and-seek behind the trees,—
　　Then plucked these roses.

Louise was one,—light, mad Louise,
But newly freed from starched decrees
　　Of school decorum ;
And Bell, the beauty, unsurprised
At fallen locks that scandalised
　　Our censor morum :—

Shy Ruth, all heart and tenderness,
Who wept—like Chaucer's Prioress—
      When Dash was smitten;
Who blushed before the mildest men,
Yet waxed a very Corday when
      You teased her kitten.

I loved them all.—Bell first and best;
Louise the next—for days of jest,
      Or madcap masking;
And Ruth, I thought,—why, failing these,
When my high-mightiness should please,
      She'd come for asking.

.   .   .   .   .

Louise was grave when last we met;
Bell's beauty, like a sun, has set;
      And Ruth, heaven bless her!
Ruth that I wooed,—and wooed in vain,
Has gone where neither grief nor pain
      Can now distress her.

TU QUOQUE:

AN IDYLL IN THE CONSERVATORY.

Austin Dobson.

"———romprons-nous,
Ou ne romprons nous pas?"
Le Dépit Amoureux.

NELLIE.

F I were you, when ladies at the play, sir,
  Beckon and nod a melodrama through,
  I would not turn abstractedly away, sir,
If I were you !

FRANK.

If I were you, when persons I affected
  Wait for three hours to take me down to Kew,
I would, at least, *pretend* I recollected,
  If I were you !

NELLIE.

If I were you, when ladies are so lavish,
  Sir, as to keep me every waltz but two,
I would not dance with *odious* Miss M'Tavish,
  If I were you !

FRANK.

If I were you, who vow you cannot suffer
  Whiff of the best, the mildest " honey-dew,"
I would not dance with smoke-consuming Puffer,
  If I were you !

NELLIE.

If I were you, I would not, sir, be bitter,
  Even to write the *Cynical Review :*—

FRANK.

No, I should doubtless find flirtation fitter,
  If I were you !

NELLIE.

Really ! you would ?   Why, Frank, you 're quite
    delightful !
Hot as Othello, and as black of hue ;—

Borrow my fan,—I would not look so *frightful*,
 If I were you !

FRANK.

"It is the cause,"—I mean, your chaperone is
 Bringing some well-curled juvenile. Adieu !
I shall retire. I 'd spare that poor Adonis,
 If I were you !

NELLIE.

Go, if you will—at once—and by express, sir !
 Where shall it be ? To China, or Peru?—
Go ! I should leave inquirers my address, sir,
 If I were you !

FRANK.

No, I remain. To stay and fight a duel
 Seems, on the whole, the proper thing to do.
Ah ! you are strong,—I would not then be cruel,
 If I were you !

NELLIE.

One does not like one's feelings to be doubted.

FRANK.

One does not like one's friends to misconstrue.

NELLIE.

If I confess that I a wee bit pouted?—

FRANK.

I should admit that I was *piqué,* too.

NELLIE.

Ask me to dance.   I'd say no more about it,
  If I were you!

[*Waltz—exeunt.*

"*G O O D - N I G H T.*"

[*Extract.*]

EDWARD FITZGERALD.

GOOD-NIGHT to thee, lady! though many
   Have joined in the dance of to-night,
Thy form was the fairest of any,
   Where all was seducing and bright ;
Thy smile was the softest and dearest,
   Thy form the most sylph-like of all,
And thy voice the most gladsome and clearest
   That e'er held a partner in thrall.

Good-night to thee, lady ! 'tis over—
   The waltz, the quadrille, and the song—

The whispered farewell of the lover,
  The heartless *adieux* of the throng;
The heart that was throbbing with pleasure,
  The eyelid that longed for repose—
The beaux that were dreaming of treasure,
  The girls that were dreaming of beaux.

'Tis over—the lights are all dying,
  The coaches all driving away;
And many a fair one is sighing,
  And many a false one is gay;
And Beauty counts over her numbers
  Of conquests, as homeward she drives—
And some are gone home to their slumbers,
  And some are gone home to their wives.

And I, while my cab in the shower
  Is waiting, the last at the door,
Am looking all round for the flower
  That fell from your wreath on the floor.

I 'll keep it—if but to remind me,
   Though withered and faded its hue—
Wherever next season may find me—
   Of England—of Almack's—and you !

IRISH EYES.

Alfred Perceval Graves.

IRISH eyes ! Irish eyes !
    Eyes that most of all can move me !
        Lift one look
        From my book,
    Through your lashes dark, and prove me
In my worship, oh how wise !

Other orbs, be content !
    In your honour, not dispraisal—
        Most I prize
        Irish eyes,
    Since were not your ebon, hazel,
Violet—all to light them lent ?

Then no mischief, merry eyes !
Stars of thought, no jealous fancies
Can I err
To prefer
This sweet union of your glances,
Sparkling, darkling Irish eyes?

AN IRISH GRACE.

Alfred Perceval Graves.

FOR beauty's blaze
  Let Pagans praise
    The features of Aglaia,
Admire agape
The maiden shape
    Consummate in Thalia,
Last hail in thee,
Euphrosyne,
    Allied the sov'ran powers
Of form and face—
No heathen Grace
    Can match this Grace of ours.

Blue are her eyes, as though the skies
  Were ever blue above them,
And dark their full-fringed canopies,
  As if the night-fays wove them.

Two roses kiss to mould her mouth,
  Her ear's a lily blossom,
Her blush a sunset in the south,
  And drifted snow her bosom.

Her voice is gay, but soft and low,
  The sweetest of all trebles,
A silver brook, that in its flow,
  Chimes over pearly pebbles.

A happy heart, a temper bright,
  Her radiant smile expresses;
And, like a wealth of golden light,
  Rain down her sunny tresses.

Earth's desert clime,

Whose sands are Time,

 Will prove a glad oasis,

If 'tis my fate,

My friends, to mate

 With such a girl as Grace is.

A BIRTHDAY IN JUNE.

Ethel Grey.

WHEN the summer sunshine gleams,
    And the warm world smiles and dreams
        All around;
When the starry roses throw
Wealth of petals' scented snow
        On the ground;

When amid sweet sounds and sights,
Full of exquisite delights,
        Fly the hours;
Comes thy birthday—rightly, dear,
For it made thee thus appear
        With the flowers.

Greeting to my fair pale rose
In these verses I enclose,
      Short and sweet;
And I lay my love so true
(Though she knows that's nothing new)
      At her feet.

And I pen these lines to-day,
Hoping she will sweetly say,
      Reading this :—
" If the writer were but here,
I would pay them all too dear,
      With a kiss ! "

A VALENTINE.

ETHEL GREY.

WELL, yes, of course it must be so ;
  No argument can shake it—
If one *will* offer up a heart,
  The other need but take it.
The truth of proverbs thus we learn,
  The notion 's far from new :
" Il y en a toujours l'un qui baise,
  Et l'autre qui tend la joue."

You may not think it fair, perhaps ;
  Indeed, it does seem funny,
That bees should have to do the work
  For drones to eat the honey ;

And yet in love 'tis just the same,
　　It is the "rule of two,"—
"Il y en a toujours l'un qui baise,
　　Et l'autre qui tend la joue."

Perhaps 'tis this unequal yoke
　　That keeps our love from dying;
One only listens to the sighs,
　　The other does the sighing.
He gives his love, his life, his hopes,—
　　She gives her smiles,—a few . . .
"Il y en a toujours l'un qui baise,
　　Et l'autre qui tend la joue."

Still, I would be content to know
　　My love had small returning;
If I could hope to warm *your* heart,
　　I would not grudge *mine* burning!
In fact, you see, it comes to this
　　(Which proves I care for you),
"Je veux être toujours l'un qui baise,
　　Si tu me tends la joue!"

"*FRUIT.*"

[*Suggested by a Picture.*]

ETHEL GREY.

AS she stands in the sunshine that streams
　　In a flood, on the sea and the land,
　A dark maiden daintily dreams
　　O'er the grape-bunch she holds in her hand.

She is ruddy, and rounded, and ripe,
　　And the clusters are fit for a show,—
She's a mouth of a classical type,—
　　Do you think she will eat them, or no?

"*SYMPATHY.*"

Reginald Heber.

A KNIGHT and a lady once met in a grove
 While each was in quest of a fugitive love;
 A river ran mournfully murmuring by,
And they wept in its waters for sympathy.

"Oh, never was knight such a sorrow that bore!"
"Oh, never was maid so deserted before!"
"From life and its woes let us instantly fly,
And jump in together for company!"

They searched for an eddy that suited the deed,
But here was a bramble, and there was a weed;
"How tiresome it is!" said the fair with a sigh;
So they sat down to rest them in company.

They gazed at each other, the maid and the knight;
How fair was her form, and how goodly his height!
"One mournful embrace," sobbed the youth, "ere we
　　die!"
So kissing and crying kept company.

"Oh, had I but loved such an angel as you!"
"Oh, had but my swain been a quarter as true!"
"To miss such perfection how blinded was I!"
Sure now they were excellent company!

At length spoke the lass, 'twixt a smile and a tear,
"The weather is cold for a watery bier;
When summer returns we may easily die,
Till then let us sorrow in company."

THE LAST LEAF.

O. W. HOLMES.

I SAW him once before,
As he passed by the door,
And again
The pavement stones resound,
As he totters o'er the ground
With his cane.

They say that in his prime,
Ere the pruning-knife of Time
Cut him down,
Not a better man was found
By the crier on his round
Through the town.

But now he walks the streets,
And he looks at all he meets
  Sad and wan,
And he shakes his feeble head,
That it seems as if he said,
  " They are gone ! "

The mossy marbles rest
On the lips that he has prest
  In their bloom ;
And the names he loved to hear
Have been carved for many a year
  On the tomb.

My grandmamma has said—
Poor old lady ! she is dead
  Long ago—
That he had a Roman nose,
And his cheek was like a rose
  In the snow.

But now his nose is thin,
And it rests upon his chin
      Like a staff;
And a crook is in his back,
And a melancholy crack
      In his laugh.

I know it is a sin
For me to sit and grin
      At him here;
But the old three-cornered hat,
And the breeches, and all that,
      Are so queer!

And if I should live to be
The last leaf upon the tree
      In the spring,
Let them smile as I do now,
At the old forsaken bough
      Where I cling.

DAILY TRIALS.

O. W. HOLMES.

H, there are times,
    When all this fret and tumult that we hear
    Do seem more stale than to the sexton's ear
His own dull chimes.

Ding dong ! ding dong !
    The world is in a simmer like a sea
    Over a pent volcano—woe is me,
All the day long !

From crib to shroud !
    Nurse o'er our cradle screameth lullaby,
    And friends in boots tramp round us as we die,
Snuffling aloud.

At morning's call
    The small-voiced pug-dog welcomes in the
        sun,
    And flea-bit mongrels, wakening one by one,
Give answer all.

When evening dim
    Draws round us, then the lonely caterwaul,
    Tart solo, sour duet, and general squall,—
These are our hymn.

Women, with tongues
    Like polar needles, ever on the jar,—
    Men, plugless word-spouts, whose deep foun-
        tains are
Within their lungs.

Children, with drums
    Strapped round them by the fond paternal ass,—
    Peripatetics with a blade of grass
Between their thumbs.

Vagrants, whose arts
    Have caged some devil in their mad machine,
    Which grinding, squeaks, with husky groans
        between,
Come out by starts.

Cockneys, that kill
    Thin horses of a Sunday,—men with clams,
    Hoarse as young bisons roaring for their dams
From hill to hill.

Soldiers, with guns,
    Making a nuisance of the blessed air,—
    Child-crying bellmen,—children in despair,
Screeching for buns.

Storms, thunders, waves !
    Howl, crash, and bellow till ye get your fill ;
    Ye sometimes rest ; men never can be still
But in their graves !

MY AUNT.

O. W. HOLMES.

MY aunt ! my dear unmarried aunt !
    Long years have o'er her flown ;
    Yet still she strains the aching clasp
That binds her virgin zone ;
I know it hurts her,—though she looks
    As cheerful as she can ;
Her waist is ampler than her life,
    For life is but a span.

My aunt ! my poor deluded aunt !
    Her hair is almost gray :
Why will she train that winter curl
    In such a spring-like way ?

How can she lay her glasses down,
　　And say she reads as well,
When, through a double convex lens,
　　She just makes out to spell?

Her father,—grandpapa! forgive
　　This erring lip its smiles,—
Vowed she should make the finest girl
　　Within a hundred miles;
He sent her to a stylish school;
　　'Twas in her thirteenth June;
And with her, as the rules required,
　　" Two towels and a spoon."

They braced my aunt against a board,
　　To make her straight and tall;
They laced her up, they starved her down,
　　To make her light and small;
They pinched her feet, they singed her hair,
　　They screwed it up with pins;—
Oh, never mortal suffered more
　　In penance for her sins.

So, when my precious aunt was done,
  My grandsire brought her back ;
(By daylight, lest some rabid youth
  Might follow in the track;)
" Ah !" said my grandsire, as he shook
  Some powder in his pan,
" What could this lovely creature do
  Against a desperate man !"

Alas ! nor chariot, nor barouche,
  Nor bandit cavalcade,
Tore from the trembling father's arms
  His all-accomplished maid.
For her how happy had it been !
  And heaven had spared to me
To see one sad, ungathered rose
  On my ancestral tree.

LINES IN A YOUNG LADY'S ALBUM.

THOMAS HOOD, SEN.

PRETTY task, Miss S——, to ask
    A Benedictine pen,
    That cannot quite at freedom write
  Like those of other men.
No lover's plaint my Muse must paint
  To fill this page's span,
But be correct and recollect
  I 'm not a single man.

Pray only think for pen and ink
  How hard to get along,
That may not turn on words that burn,
  Or Love, the life of song !

Nine Muses, if I chooses, I
 May woo all in a clan,
But one Miss S—— I daren't address—
 I 'm not a single man.

Scribblers unwed, with little head
 May eke it out with heart,
And in their lays it often plays
 A rare first-fiddle part:
They make a kiss to rhyme with bliss,
 But if *I* so began,
I have my fears about my ears—
 I 'm not a single man.

Upon your cheek I may not speak,
 Nor on your lip be warm,
I must be wise about your eyes,
 And formal with your form;
Of all that sort of thing, in short,
 On T. H. Bayly's plan,
I must not twine a single line—
 I 'm not a single man.

A watchman's part compels my heart
  To keep you off its *beat,*
And I might dare as soon to swear
  At *you* as at your feet.
I can't expire in passion's fire,
  As other poets can—
My life (she 's by) won't let me die—
  I 'm not a single man.

Shut out from love, denied a dove,
  Forbidden bow and dart,
Without a groan to call my own,
  With neither hand nor heart,
To Hymen vowed, and not allowed
  To flirt e'en with your fan,
Here end, as just a friend, I must—
  I 'm not a single man.

TO MINERVA.

Thomas Hood, Sen.

MY temples throb, my pulses boil,
    I'm sick of song, and ode, and ballad,—
So Thyrsis, take the midnight oil,
    And pour it on a lobster-salad.

My brain is dull, my sight is foul,
    I cannot write a verse, or read,—
Then Pallas take away thine owl,
    And let us have a lark instead.

"*PLEASE TO RING THE BELLE.*"

Thomas Hood, Sen.

I'LL tell you a story that's not in Tom Moore:
Young Love likes to knock at a pretty girl's door:
So he called upon Lucy—'twas just ten o'clock—
Like a spruce single man, with a smart double knock.

Now a hand-maid, whatever her fingers be at,
Will run like a puss when she hears a *rat*-tat:
So Lucy ran up—and in two seconds more
Had questioned the stranger and answered the door.

The meeting was bliss ; but the parting was woe ;

For the moment will come when such comers must go.

So she kissed him, and whispered—poor innocent

 thing—

" The next time you come, love, pray come with a

 ring."

THE TIME OF ROSES.

Thomas Hood, Sen.

IT was not in the winter
  Our loving lot was cast ;
It was the time of roses,—
  We plucked them as we passed.

That churlish season never frowned
  On early lovers yet :
Oh, no ! the world was newly crowned
  With flowers when first we met !

'Twas twilight, and I bade you go,
  But still you held me fast ;
It was the time of roses,—
  We plucked them as we passed.

What else could peer thy glowing cheek,
    That tears began to stud?
And when I asked the like of Love,
    You snatched a damask bud;

And oped it to the dainty core,
    Still glowing to the last.
It was the time of roses,—
    We plucked them as we passed.

L.

GRETCHEN.

A Leaf from an Artist's Sketch-Book.

Thomas Hood, Jun.

GRETCHEN comes from over the sea,
  From the land where clusters purple the vine
  On the sunny slopes that rise from the Rhine,
    As blue as my Gretchen's e'e!

Down by the ocean's brim we met,
  In a bay embosomed in gleaming sand,
  With a headland stark upon either hand,
    While the sun before us set.

Golden light upon golden locks,
  By pools of emerald broidered with pearl,

Where the waters broke with a sweep and
swirl,
To whisper amid the rocks.

I drew her face in my treasure-book—
Artists have licenses; this is one!—
As she stood in the light of the sinking sun;
And here it is:—you may look!

She went east—and I went west;
But I bear her image wherever I go.
One is here in my sketch-book, lo!
Another within my breast.

LITTLE FAN.

Thomas Hood, Jun.

OUR Fan is a fairy, as funny as Puck,
   In all sorts of innocent mischief for ever.
We think she's a changeling;—but ah! by
    good luck,
She's not ugly and crafty, but pretty and clever!
Go search through all elfdom, and find if you can
A fay half as fair as our frolicsome Fan.

She has opened the door for the magpie, you see;
   And Mag has set out on a mission of plunder!
Miss Mischief!—'twas sympathy set the bird free.
   You deserve it—yet ah! who could chide you, I
    wonder?

Why, a touch spoils a butterfly's wing ;—not *my*
    plan ;
Though I fear that I'm spoiling you, frolicsome
    Fan !

ALL IN THE DOWNS.

Thomas Hood, Jun.

"Had I a little son, I would christen him ' Nothing-to-do.'"
Charles Lamb.

WOULD I had something to do—or to think !
  Or something to read, or to write !
I am rapidly verging on lunacy's brink,
  Or I shall be dead before night.

In my ears has been ringing and droning all day,
  Without ever a stop or a change,
That poem of Tennyson's—heart-cheering lay !—
Of the moated monotonous Grange !

The stripes in the carpet and paper alike
   I have counted, and counted all through,
And now I 've a fervid ambition to strike
   Out some path of wild pleasure that 's new.

They say, if a number you count, and recount,
   That the time imperceptibly goes,—
Ah! I wish—how I wish!—I'd ne'er learnt the amount
   Of my aggregate fingers and toes.

" Enjoyment is fleeting," the proverbs all say,
   " Even that which it feeds upon fails."
I 've arrived at the truth of the saying to-day,
   By devouring the whole of my nails.

I have numbered the minutes so heavy and slow,
   Till of that dissipation I tire,
And as for exciting amusements,—you know
   One can't *always* be stirring the fire.

THE BRACELET.

(From Abroad.)

Thomas Hood, Jun.

TAKE, dearest one, this golden band,
   And clasp it round thine arm for me—
Who fain would link with mine own hand
   This token of my life to thee.

Oh, may thy pulse beneath it beat
   One measured rhythm with thy heart,
Beat quick with joy, love, when we meet—
   And only slowly when we part.

And may thy moments, free from pain,
   And full of joy, pass calmly by—
Links, dearest, of a silver chain,—
   Beads, in a golden rosary!

R O N D E A U.

Leigh Hunt.

JENNY kissed me when we met,
  Jumping from the chair she sat in ;
Time, you thief, who love to get
Sweets into your list, put *that* in :
Say I 'm weary, say I 'm sad,
  Say that health and wealth have missed me,
Say I 'm growing old, but add,
  Jenny kissed me !

A LOVE-LESSON.

LEIGH HUNT.

 SWEET "No, no,"—with a sweet smile beneath,
    Becomes an honest girl; I 'd have you learn
    it :—
As for plain " Yes," it may be said i' faith,
    Too plainly and too oft :—pray, well discern it—

Not that I 'd have my pleasure incomplete,
    Or lose the kiss for which my lips beset you ;
But that in suffering me to take it, Sweet,
    I 'd have you say, " No, no, I will not let you."

LOVE AND AGE.

LEIGH HUNT.

WHEN young, I loved. At that enchanting
age,
So sweet, so short, love was my sole delight;
And when I reached the time for being sage,
Still I loved on, for reason gave me right.

Snows come at length, and livelier joys depart,
Yet gentle ones still kiss these eyelids dim;
For still I love, and love consoles my heart;
What could console me for the loss of *Him?*

LETTICE WHITE.

JEAN INGELOW.

MY neighbour White; we met to-day,
　　He always had a cheerful way,
　　　　As if he breathed at ease ;
My neighbour White lives down the glade,
And I live higher, in the shade
　　　　Of my old walnut-trees.

So many lads and lasses small,
To feed them all, to clothe them all,
　　　　Must surely tax his wit ;
I see his thatch when I look out,
His branching roses creep about
　　　　And vines half smother it.

There white-haired urchins climb his eaves,
And little watch-fires heap with leaves,
    And milky filberts hoard ;
And there his oldest daughter stands
With downcast eyes and skilful hands
    Before her ironing-board.

She comforts all her mother's days,
And with her sweet obedient ways
    She makes her labours light ;
So sweet to hear, so fair to see !
Oh, she is much too good for me,
    That lovely Lettice White !

'Tis hard to feel one's self a fool !
With that same lass I went to school ;
    I then was great and wise ;
She read upon an easier book,
And I,—I never cared to look
    Into her shy blue eyes.

And now I know they must be there,
Sweet eyes, behind those lashes fair
　　That will not raise their rim :
If maids be shy, he cures who can,
But if a man be shy—a man—
　　Why then, the worse for him !

My mother cries, "For such a lad
A wife is easy to be had
　　And always to be found ;
A finer scholar scarce can be,
And for a foot and leg," says she,
　　" He beats the country round !"

" My handsome boy must stoop his head
To clear her door whom he would wed."
　　Weak praise, but fondly sung !
" O mother ! scholars sometimes fail,---
And what can foot and leg avail
　　To him that wants a tongue !"

When by her ironing-board I sit
Her little sisters round me flit,
  And bring me forth their store;
Dark cluster grapes of dusty blue,
And small sweet apples bright of hue,
  And crimson to the core.

But she abideth silent, fair,
All shaded by her flaxen hair,
  The blushes come and go;
I look, and I no more can speak
Than the red sun that on her cheek
  Smiles as he lieth low.

Sometimes the roses by the latch
Or scarlet vine leaves from her thatch
  Come sailing down like birds;
When from their drifts her board I clear,
She thanks me, but I scarce can hear
  The shyly uttered words.

Oft have I wooed sweet Lettice White
By daylight and by candlelight
　　When we two were apart.
Some better day come on apace,
And let me tell her face to face,
　　　"Maiden, thou hast my heart!"

How gently rock yon poplars high
Against the reach of primrose sky
　　With heaven's pale candles stored!
She sees them all, sweet Lettice White;
　'll e'en go sit again to-night
　　　Beside her ironing-board.

THE POPLAR.

Thomas Ingoldsby.

AY, here stands the Poplar, so tall and so
    stately,
  On whose tender rind—'twas a little one
    then—
We carved her initials; though not very lately—
  We think in the year eighteen hundred and ten.

Yes, here is the *G* which proclaimed Georgiana,
  Our heart's empress then; see, 'tis grown all
    askew;
And it's not without grief we perforce entertain a
  Conviction, it now looks much more like a *Q*.

M

This should be the great *D*, too, that once stood for
    Dobbin,
  Her loved patronymic—ah! can it be so?
Its once fair proportions, time, too, has been robbing
  A *D* ?—we'll be Deed if it isn't an *O* /

Alas! how the soul sentimental it vexes,
    That thus on our labours stern Chronos should
      frown,
Should change our soft liquids to izzards and X'es,
    And turn true-love's alphabet all upside down!*

* Reprinted from " Ingoldsby Legends," by permission of
Messrs Richard Bentley & Son.

SING HEIGH-HO!

REV. CHARLES KINGSLEY.

THERE sits a bird on every tree,
　　Sing heigh-ho !
There sits a bird on every tree,
And courts his love, as I do thee ;
　　Sing heigh-ho, and heigh-ho !
Young maids must marry.—

There grows a flower on every bough,
　　Sing heigh-ho !
There grows a flower on every bough,
Its petals kiss—I 'll show you how :
　　Sing heigh-ho, and heigh-ho !
Young maids must marry.

From sea to stream the salmon roam :
    Sing heigh-ho !
From sea to stream the salmon roam ;
Each finds a mate, and leads her home ;
    Sing heigh-ho, and heigh-ho !
Young maids must marry.

The sun 's a bridegroom, earth a bride
    Sing heigh-ho !
They court from morn till eventide :
The earth shall pass, but love abide ;
    Sing heigh-ho, and heigh-ho !
Young maids must marry.

THE EFFECTS OF AGE.

WALTER SAVAGE LANDOR.

YES, I write verses now and then,
　　But blunt and flaccid is my pen,
　　No longer talked of by young men
　　　　As rather clever.
In their last quarter are my eyes,
You see it by their form and size,
Is it not time, then, to be wise?—
　　　　Or now, or never.

Fairest that ever sprang from Eve!
While time allows the short reprieve
Just look at me! Could you believe
　　　　'Twas once a lover?

I cannot clear the five-barred gate,
But trying first its timber's state,
Climb stiffly up, take breath and wait,
   To trundle over.

Through galopade I cannot swing
Th' entangling blooms of beauty's spring ;
I cannot say the tender thing,
   Be 't true or false.
And am beginning to opine
Those girls are only half divine
Whose waists you wicked boys entwine
   In giddy waltz.

I fear that arm above that shoulder,
I wish them wiser, graver, older,
Sedater, and no harm if colder,
   And panting less.
Ah ! people were not half so wild
In former days, when, starchly mild,
Upon her high-heeled Essex smiled
   The brave Queen Bess.

THE PORTRAIT-PAINTER.

Walter Savage Landor.

THOU whose happy pencil strays
　　Where I am called, nor dare to gaze,
　　　　But lower my eye and check my tongue,
Oh, if thou valuest peaceful days,
Pursue the ringlet's sunny maze,
　　　　And dwell not on those lips too long.

What mists athwart my temples fly,
Now, touch by touch, thy fingers tie
　　　　With torturing care her graceful zone !
For all that sparkles from her eye
I could not look while thou art by,
　　　　Nor could I cease were I alone.

HIGH AND DRY.

Walter Savage Landor.

THE vessel that rests here at last
    Had once stout ribs and topping mast,
    And, whate'er wind there might prevail,
Was ready for a row or sail;
It now lies idle on its side,
Forgetful o'er the stream to glide.
And yet there have been days of yore
When pretty maids their posies bore
To crown its prow, its deck to trim,
And freighted a whole world of whim.
A thousand stories it could tell,
But it loves secrecy too well.
Come closer, my sweet girl, pray do ! . . . .
There may be still one left for you.

COMMINATION.

WALTER SAVAGE LANDOR.

AKING my walk the other day,
    I saw a little girl at play,
    So pretty, 'twould not be amiss,
Thought I, to venture on a kiss.
Fiercely the little girl began—
" *I wonder at you, nasty man !*"
And all four fingers were applied,
And crimson pinafore beside,
To wipe what venom might remain,—
" *Do if you dare the like again ;*
I have a mind to teach you better,"
And I too had a mind to let her.

NO LONGER JEALOUS.

WALTER SAVAGE LANDOR.

I REMEMBER the time ere his temples were grey,
And I frowned at the things he 'd the boldness
to say ;
But now he 's grown old, he may say what he will,
I laugh at his nonsense and take nothing ill.

Indeed I must say he 's a little improved,
For he watches no longer the ' slily beloved,'
No longer as once he awakens my fears,
Not a glance he perceives, not a whisper he hears.

If he heard one of late, it has never transpired,
For his only delight is to see me admired ;
And now pray what better return can I make,
Than to flirt and be always admired—for his sake.

DEFIANCE.

WALTER SAVAGE LANDOR.

CATCH her and hold her if you can !
See, she defies you with her fan,
Shuts, opens, and then holds it spread
In threat'ning guise above your head.
Ah! why did you not start before
She reached the porch and closed the door?
Simpleton! will you never learn
That girls and time will not return ;
Of each you should have made the most,
Once gone, they are for ever lost.
In vain your knuckles knock your brow,
In vain will you remember how
Like a slim brook the gamesome maid
Sparkled, and ran into the shade.

THERE'S A TIME TO BE JOLLY.

CHARLES G. LELAND (*Hans Breitmann*).

HERE'S a time to be jolly, a time to repent,
A season for folly, a season for Lent,
The first as the worst we too often regard;
The rest as the best, but our judgment is hard.

There are snows in December and roses in June,
There's darkness at midnight and sunshine at noon;
But, were there no sorrow, no storm-cloud or rain,
Who'd care for the morrow with beauty again.

The world is a picture both gloomy and bright,
And grief is the shadow and pleasure the light,
And neither should smother the general tone:
For where were the other if either were gone?

The valley is lovely ; the mountain is drear,
Its summit is hidden in mist all the year ;
But gaze from the heaven, high over all weather,
And mountain and valley are lovely together.

I have learned to love Lucy, though faded she be ;
If my next love be lovely, the better for me.
By the end of next summer, I 'll give you my oath,
It was best, after all, to have flirted with both.

WHAT MIGHT HAVE BEEN.

HENRY S. LEIGH.

IN the twilight of November's
    Afternoons I like to sit,
  Finding fancies in the embers
  Long before my lamp is lit;
Calling memory up, and linking
    Bygone days to distant scene;
Then, with feet on fender, thinking
    Of the things that might have been.

  Cradles, wedding-rings, and hatchments
    Glow alternate in the fire;
  Early loves, and late attachments
    Blaze a second,—and expire.

With a moderate persistence
  One may soon contrive to glean
Matters for a mock existence
  From the things that might have been.

Handsome, amiable, and clever—
  With a fortune and a wife :—
So I make my start whenever
  I would build the fancy life.
After all the bright ideal,
  What a gulf there is between
Things that are, alas ! too real,
  And the things that might have been !

Often thus, alone and moody,
  Do I act my little play—
Like a ghostly Punch and Judy,
  Where the dolls are grave and gay ;—
Till my lamplight comes and flashes
  On the phantoms I have seen,
Leaving nothing but the ashes
  Of the things that might have been.

A CLUMSY SERVANT.

HENRY S. LEIGH.

NATURE, Nature, you 're enough
　To put a Quaker in a huff,
　　Or make a martyr grumble !
Whenever something rich and rare—
On earth—at sea—or in the air—
Is placed in your especial care,
　　You always let it tumble.

You don't, like other folks, confine
Your fractures to the hardware line,
　　And break the trifles *they* break ;
But, scorning anything so small,
You take our nights and let them fall,
And in the morning, worst of all,
　　You go and let the day break !

You drop the rains of early spring
(That set the wide world blossoming),
   The golden beams that mellow
Our grain toward the harvest prime ;
You drop, too, in the autumn-time,
With breathings from a colder clime,
   The dead leaf, sere and yellow.

You drop and drop ;—without a doubt
You 'll go on dropping things about,
   Through still and stormy weather,
Until a day when you shall find
You feel aweary of mankind,
And end by making up your mind
   To drop us altogether.

A BEGGING LETTER.

HENRY S. LEIGH.

MY DEAR TO-MORROW,
                    I can think
    Of little else to do,
And so I take my pen and ink
    And drop a line to you.
I own that I am ill at ease
    Respecting you to-day;
Do let me have an answer, please;
    Répondez, s'il vous plaît.

I long to like you very much,
    But that will all depend
On whether you " behave as such "
    (I mean, dear, as a friend).

I 'll set you quite an easy task
    At which you are *au fait;*
You 'll come and bring me what I ask?
    Répondez, s'il vous plaît.

Be sure to recollect your purse,
    For, be it understood,
Though money-matters might be worse,
    They 're very far from good.
So, if you have a little gold
    You care to give away——
But am I growing over-bold?
    Répondez, s'il vous plaît.

A little—just a little—fame
    You must contrive to bring;
Because I think a poet's name
    Would be a pleasant thing.
Perhaps, though, as I 've scarcely got
    A single claim to lay
To such a gift, you 'd rather not;
    Répondez, s'il vous plaît.

Well, well, To-morrow, you may strike
　　A line through what's above:
And bring me folks that I can like,
　　And folks that I can love.
A warmer heart; a quicker brain,
　　I'll ask for, if I may:
To-morrow, shall I ask in vain?
　　Répondez, s'il vous plaît.

MY LOVE AND MY HEART.

HENRY S. LEIGH.

OH, the days were ever shiny
　　When I ran to meet my love;
　When I pressed her hand so tiny
Through her tiny, tiny glove.
Was I very deeply smitten?
　Oh, I loved like *anything!*
But my love she is a kitten,
　And my heart's a ball of string.

She was pleasingly poetic,
　And she loved my little rhymes;
For our tastes were sympathetic,
　In the old and happy times.

Oh, the ballads I have written,
  And have taught my love to sing ! . . .
But my love she is a kitten,
  And my heart 's a ball of string.

Would she listen to my offer,
  On my knees I would impart
A sincere and ready proffer
  Of my hand and of my heart.
And below her dainty mitten
  I would fix a wedding-ring ;
But my love she is a kitten,
  And my heart 's a ball of string.

Take a warning, happy lover,
  From the moral that I show ;
Or too late you may discover
  What I learned a month ago,
We are scratched or we are bitten
  By the pets to whom we cling,—
Oh, my love she is a kitten,
  And my heart 's a ball of string.

MY PARTNER.

Henry S. Leigh.

FULL often at my cosy club
    I take my claret and my joint,
And then essay a friendly rub
At silver threepennies the point.
My partner is a ghastly man,
    With awful knowledge of the game;
And—play as deftly as I can—
    He treats my efforts all the same.

I lead a trump, no matter why—
    We lose the trick, no matter how;
I feel the fury of his eye,
    And see the scowl upon his brow.

I give a shrug, as if to say,
  'Twas purely an affair of chance ;
He coughs in quite a quiet way—
  But, oh, the lightning of his glance !

Perchance I play a lively king,
  When swiftly on the monarch's face
(Before I dream of such a thing)
  My bold opponent puts an ace.
The luck is theirs, and such a tide
  Is quite impossible to stem ;
My partner turns his head aside,
  And mournfully observes, " Ahem ! "

At length I gradually lose
  All sense of what we are about ;
With little time to pick or choose,
  I play a card when twelve are out.
I know it 's utterly absurd,
  And frankly feel we cannot win ;
My partner never says a word,
  But kicks me hard upon the shin.

What matters that?   One little graze
    Will only last a week or so ;
And what are six or seven days
    Of poulticing to undergo?
But, when I wildly dash away,
    More desperately than before,
My partner swears he 'll never play
    With such an idiot any more.

NOT A MATCH.

HENRY S. LEIGH.

ITTY, sweet and seventeen,
  Pulls my hair and calls me "Harry;"
Hints that I am young and green,
Wonders if I wish to marry.
Only tell me what reply
  Is the best reply for Kitty?
She 's but seventeen—and *I*—
  I am forty—more 's the pity.

Twice at least my Kitty's age
  (Just a trifle over, maybe)—
I am sober, I am sage ;
  Kitty nothing but a baby.

She is merriment and mirth,
  I am wise and gravely witty;
She 's the dearest thing on earth,
  I am forty—more 's the pity.

She adores my pretty rhymes,
  Calls me " poet " when I write them;
And she listens oftentimes
  Half an hour when I recite them.
Let me scribble by the page
  Sonnet, ode, or lover's ditty;
Seventeen is Kitty's age—
  I am forty—more 's the pity.

TO MY GRANDMOTHER.

[Suggested by a Picture by Mr Romney.]

FREDERICK LOCKER.

HIS relative of mine
    Was she seventy-and-nine
        When she died?
By the canvas may be seen
How she looked at seventeen
        As a bride.

Beneath a summer tree
Her maiden reverie
        Has a charm;
Her ringlets are in taste—
What an arm! and what a waist
        For an arm!

With her bridal-wreath, bouquet,
Lace farthingale, and gay
    Falbala,—
Were Romney's limning true,
What a lucky dog were you,
    Grandpapa!

Her lips are sweet as love ;
They are parting ! do they move ?
    Are they dumb ?
Her eyes are blue, and beam
Beseechingly, and seem
    To say, " Come ! "

What funny fancy slips
From atween these cherry lips !
    Whisper me,
Sweet deity in paint,
What canon says I mayn't
    Marry thee ?

That good-for-nothing Time
Has a confidence sublime !
     When I first
Saw this lady in my youth,
Her winters had, forsooth,
     Done their worst.

Her locks (as white as snow)
Once shamed the swarthy crow :
     By-and-by,
That fowl's avenging sprite
Set his cruel foot for spite
     Near her eye.

Her rounded form was lean,
And her silk was bambazine :
     Well I wot
With her needles would she sit,
And for hours would she knit,—
     Would she not ?

Ah, perishable clay !
Her charms had dropt away
    One by one.
But if she heaved a sigh
With a burthen, it was, " Thy
    Will be done."

In travail, as in tears,
With the fardel of her years
    Overprest,
In mercy was she borne
Where the weary and the worn
    Are at rest.

I fain would meet you there ;—
If, witching as you were,
    Grandmamma,
This nether world agrees
That the better you must please
    Grandpapa.

REPLY TO A LETTER ENCLOSING A LOCK OF HAIR.

FREDERICK LOCKER.

YES, you were false, and though I 'm free,
   I still would be the slave of yore ;
   Then, joined, our years were thirty-three,
And now,—yes, now I 'm thirty-four.
And though you were not learnèd—well,
   I was not anxious you should grow so ;—
I trembled once beneath her spell
   Whose spelling was extremely so-so !

Bright season ! Why will Memory
   Still haunt the path our rambles took,—
The sparrow's nest that made you cry,
   The lilies captured in the brook ?

I 'd lifted you from side to side
  (You seemed as light as that poor sparrow);
I know who wished it twice as wide,
  I think *you* thought it rather narrow.

Time was, indeed a little while,
  My pony could your heart compel;
And once, beside the meadow-stile,
  I thought you loved me just as well;
I 'd kissed your cheek; in sweet surprise
  Your troubled gaze said plainly, "Should he?"
But doubt soon fled those daisy eyes;—
  "He could not mean to vex me, could he?"

The brightest eyes are soonest sad,
  But your rose cheek, so lightly swayed,
Could ripple into dimples glad;
  For O, fair friend, what mirth we made!
The brightest tears are soonest dried,
  But your young love and dole were stable;

You wept when dear old Rover died,
　　You wept—and dressed your dolls in sable.

As year succeeds to year, the more
　　Imperfect life's fruition seems ;
Our dreams, as baseless as of yore,
　　Are not the same enchanting dreams.
The girls I love now vote me slow—
　　How dull the boys who once seemed witty !
Perhaps I 'm getting old, I know
　　I 'm still romantic, more 's the pity !

Vain the regret ! to few, perchance,
　　Unknown, and profitless to all ;
The wisely-gay, as years advance,
　　Are gaily wise.　Whate'er befall,
We 'll laugh at folly, whether seen
　　Beneath a chimney or a steeple ;
At yours, at mine—our own, I mean,
　　As well as that of other people.

I 'm fond of fun, the mental dew
　　Where wit, and truth, and ruth are blent ;

And yet I 've known a prig or two,
　Who, wanting all, were all content !
To say I hate such dismal men
　Might be esteemed a strong assertion ;
If I 've blue devils, now and then,
　I make them dance for my diversion. . . .

And here 's your letter débonnaire,
　" My friend, my dear old friend of yore,"
And is this curl your daughter's hair?
　I 've seen the Titian tint before.
Are we the pair that used to pass
　Long days beneath the chestnut shady?
Then you were such a pretty lass !
　I 'm told you 're now as fair a lady.

I 've laughed to hide the tear I shed,
　As when the jester's bosom swells,
And mournfully he shakes his head,
　We hear the jingle of his bells.

A jesting vein your poet vexed,
And this poor rhyme, the Fates determine,
Without a parson or a text,
Has proved a somewhat prosy sermon.

MY NEIGHBOUR ROSE.

FREDERICK LOCKER.

THOUGH walls but thin our hearths divide,
   We 're strangers dwelling side by side ;
   How gaily all your days must glide
      Unvexed by labour !
I 've seen you weep, and could have wept ;
I 've heard you sing (and might have slept !)
Sometimes I hear your chimney swept,
      My charming neighbour !

Your pets are mine.   Pray what may ail
The pup, once eloquent of tail?
I wonder why your nightingale
      Is mute at sunset !

Your puss, demure and pensive, seems
Too fat to mouse.   Much she esteems
Yon sunny wall, and, dozing, dreams
        Of mice she once ate.

Our tastes agree.   I dote upon
Frail jars, turquoise and celadon,
The *Wedding March* of Mendelssohn,
        And *Penseroso*.
When sorely tempted to purloin
Your *pietà* of Marc Antoine,
Fair virtue doth fair play enjoin,
        Fair Virtuoso !

At times an Ariel, cruel-kind,
Will kiss my lips, and stir your blind,
And whisper low, " She hides behind ;
        Thou art not lonely."
The tricksy sprite did erst assist
At hushed Verona's moonlight tryst ;—
Sweet Capulet ! thou wert not kissed
        By light winds only.

I miss the simple days of yore,
When two long braids of hair you wore,
And *Chat botté* was wondered o'er,
      In corner cosy.
But gaze not back for tales like those :
It's all in order, I suppose,
The Bud is now a blooming Rose,—
      A rosy-posy !

Indeed, farewell to bygone years ;
How wonderful the change appears !
For curates now, and cavaliers,
      In turn perplex you :
The last are birds of feather gay,
Who swear the first are birds of prey ;
I'd scare them all had I my way,
      But that might vex you.

At times I've envied, it is true,
That hero, joyous twenty-two,
Who sent *bouquets* and *billets-doux*,
      And wore a sabre.

The rogue! how close his arm he wound
About her waist, who never frowned.
He loves you, child.　Now, is he bound
　　To love *my* neighbour?

The bells are ringing.　As is meet,
White favours fascinate the street,
Sweet faces greet me, rueful-sweet
　　'Twixt tears and laughter :
They crowd the door to see her go,
The bliss of one brings many woe ;
Oh, kiss the bride, and I will throw
　　The old shoe after.

What change in one short afternoon,
My own dear neighbour gone,—so soon !
Is yon pale orb her honey-moon
　　Slow rising hither?
Lady ! so wan and marvellous,
How often have we communed thus :
Sweet memory shall dwell with us,—
　　And joy go with her !

MRS SMITH.

Frederick Locker.

LAST year I trod these fields with Di,
    Fields fresh with clover and with rye;
        They now seem arid!
Then Di was fair and single; how
Unfair it seems on me, for now
        Di's fair—and married!

A blissful swain—I scorned the song
Which says that though young Love is strong,
        The Fates are stronger:
Breezes then blew a boon to men,
Then butter-cups were bright, and then
        This grass was longer.

That day I saw, and much esteemed
Di's ankles, which the clover seemed
        Inclined to smother:
It twitched, and soon untied (for fun)
The ribbons of her shoes, first one,
        And then the other.

I 'm told that virgins augur some
Misfortune if their shoe-strings come
        To grief on Friday:
And so did Di, and so her pride
Decreed that shoe-strings so untied
        Are " so untidy!"

Of course I knelt; with fingers deft
I tied the right, and tied the left:
        Says Di, " This stubble
Is very stupid!—as I live,
I 'm quite ashamed!—I 'm shocked to give
        You so much trouble."

For answer I was fain to sink
To what we all would say and think
　　Were Beauty present :
" Don't mention such a simple act—
A trouble? not the least !—in fact
　　It's rather pleasant ! "

I trust that Love will never tease
Poor little Di, or prove that he's
　　A graceless rover.
She's happy now as *Mrs Smith*—
And less polite when walking with
　　Her chosen lover !

Heigh-ho ! although no moral clings
To Di's blue eyes, and sandal-strings,
　　We've had our quarrels !—
I think that Smith is thought an ass,
I know that when they walk in grass
　　She wears *balmorals*.

MY MISTRESS'S BOOTS.

FREDERICK LOCKER.

THEY nearly strike me dumb,
  And I tremble when they come
    Pit-a-pat:
This palpitation means
These Boots are Geraldine's—
    Think of that!

Oh, where did hunter win
So delectable a skin
    For her feet?
You lucky little kid,
You perished, so you did,
    For my sweet!

The faëry stitching gleams
On the sides, and in the seams,
> And it shows
The Pixies were the wags
Who tipt those funny tags
> And these toes.

What soles to charm an elf!
Had Crusoe, sick of self,
> Chanced to view
One printed near the tide,
Oh, how hard he would have tried
> For the two!

For Gerry's debonair
And innocent, and fair
> As a rose;
She's an angel in a frock,
With a fascinating cock
> To her nose.

The simpletons who squeeze
Their extremities to please
            Mandarins,
Would positively flinch
From venturing to pinch
            Geraldine's.

Cinderella's *lefts and rights,*
To Geraldine's were frights ;
            And I trow,
The damsel, deftly shod,
Has dutifully trod
            Until now.

Come, Gerry, since it suits
Such a pretty Puss (in Boots)
            These to don ;
Set this dainty hand awhile
On my shoulder, dear, and I 'll
            Put them on.

GERTY'S GLOVE.

FREDERICK LOCKER.

" Elle avait au bout de ses manches
Une paire de mains si blanches ! "

LIPS of a kid-skin deftly sewn,
   A scent as through her garden blown,
The tender hue that clothes her dove,
All these, and this is Gerty's glove.

A glove but lately dofft, for look—
It keeps the happy shape it took
Warm from her touch!   What gave the glow?—
And where's the mould that shaped it so?

It clasped the hand, so pure, so sleek,
Where Gerty rests a pensive cheek,
The hand that when the light wind stirs,
Reproves those laughing locks of hers.

You fingers four, you little thumb !
Were I but you, in days to come
I 'd clasp, and kiss, and keep her—go !
And tell her that I told you so.

"*GERTY'S NECKLACE.*"

FREDERICK LOCKER.

AS Gerty skipt from babe to girl,
    Her necklace lengthened, pearl by pearl;
  Year after year it grew and grew,
For every birthday gave her two.
Her neck is lovely, soft, and fair,
And now her necklace glimmers there.

So cradled, let it sink and rise,
And all her graces emblemise;
Perchance this pearl, without a speck,
Once was as warm on Sappho's neck;
And where are all the happy pearls
That braided Beatrice's curls?

P

Is Gerty loved?—is Gerty loth?
Or, if she's either, is she both?
She's fancy free, but sweeter far
Than many plighted maidens are:
Will Gerty smile us all away,
And still be Gerty?   Who can say?

But let her wear her precious toy,
And I 'll rejoice to see her joy:
Her bauble's only one degree
Less frail, less fugitive than we;
For Time, ere long, will snap the skein,
And scatter all the pearls again.

WITHOUT AND WITHIN.

J. RUSSELL LOWELL.

MY coachman, in the moonlight there,
Looks through the side-light of the door;
I hear him with his brethren swear,
As I could do,—but only more.

Flattening his nose against the pane,
He envies me my brilliant lot,
Breathes on his aching fist in vain,
And dooms me to a place more hot.

He sees me into supper go,
A silken wonder by my side,
Bare arms, bare shoulders, and a row
Of flounces, for the door too wide.

He thinks how happy is my arm,
    'Neath its white-gloved and jewelled load;
And wishes me some dreadful harm,
    Hearing the merry corks explode.

Meanwhile I inly curse the bore
    Of hunting still the same old coon,
And envy him, outside the door,
    The golden quiet of the moon.

The winter wind is not so cold
    As the bright smile he sees me win,
Nor the host's oldest wine so old
    As our poor gabble, sour and thin.

I envy him the rugged prance
    By which his freezing feet he warms,
And drag my lady's chains, and dance,
    The galley-slave of dreary forms.

Oh, could he have my share of din,

　　And I his quiet!—past a doubt

'Twould still be one man bored within,

　　And just another bored without.

"*AUF WIEDERSEHEN!*"

[*Extract.*]

J. RUSSELL LOWELL.

THE little gate was reached at last,
    Half hid in lilacs down the lane ;
    She pushed it wide, and, as she past,
A wistful look she backward cast,
    And said, " Auf wiedersehen ! "

With hand on latch, a vision white
    Lingered reluctant, and again,
Half doubting if she did aright,
Soft as the dews that fell that night,
    She said, " Auf wiedersehen ! "

The lamp's clear gleam flits up the stair ;
    I linger in delicious pain ;

Ah ! in that chamber, whose rich air
To breathe in thought I scarcely dare,
   Thinks she, " Auf wiedersehen ! "

Sweet piece of bashful maiden art !
   The English words had seemed too fain,
But these—they drew us heart to heart,
Yet held us tenderly apart ;
   She said, " Auf wiedersehen ! "

AN EMBER PICTURE.

J. Russell Lowell.

HOW strange are the freaks of memory !
　　The lessons of life we forget,
　　While a trifle, a trick of colour,
　　In the wonderful web is set,—

Set by some mordant of fancy,
　　And, spite of the wear and tear
Of time or distance or trouble,
　　Insists on its right to be there.

A chance had brought us together ;
　　Our talk was of matters of course ;
We were nothing, one to the other,
　　But a short half-hour's resource.

Arrived at her door, we left her
    With a drippingly hurried adieu,
And our wheels went crunching the gravel
    Of the oak-darkened avenue.

As we drove away through the shadow,
    The candle she held at the door
From rain-varnished tree-trunk to tree-trunk
    Flashed fainter, and flashed no more ;—

Flashed fainter, then wholly faded
    Before we had passed the wood ;
But the light of the face behind it
    Went with me and stayed for good.

.   .   .   .   .   .

Had she beauty?   Well, not what they call so ;
    You may find a thousand as fair ;
And yet there's her face in my memory
    With no special claim to be there.

As I sit sometimes in the twilight,
　And call back to life in the coals
Old faces and hopes and fancies
　Long buried (good rest to their souls!)—

Her face shines out in the embers;
　I see her holding the light,
And hear the crunch of the gravel,
　And the sweep of the rain that night.

THE FAIRY'S REPROACH.

BULWER LYTTON.

BY the glow-worm's lamp in the dewy brake ;
By the gossamer's airy net ;
By the shifting skin of the faithless snake,
Oh, teach me to forget :—
For none, ah, none,
· Can teach so well that human spell,
As thou, false one !

By the fairy dance on the greensward smooth ;
By the winds of the gentle west ;
By the loving stars, when their soft looks soothe
The waves on their mother's breast ;

Teach me thy lore,

By which, like withered flowers,

The leaves of buried hours

Blossom no more !

By the tent in the violet's bell ;

By the may on the scented bough ;

By the lone green isle where my sisters dwell ;

And thine own forgotten vow !

Teach me to live,

Nor feed on thoughts that pine

For love so false as thine !

Teach me thy lore,

And one thou lov'st no more

Will bless thee, and forgive.*

* Reprinted from " The Pilgrims of the Rhine," by permission
of Messrs George Routledge & Sons.

NYDIA'S LOVE-SONG.

BULWER LYTTON.

THE wind and the beam loved the rose,
    And the rose loved one ;
    For who recks the wind where it blows ?
Or loves not the sun ?

None knew whence the humble wind stole
    Poor sport of the skies—
None dreamt that the wind had a soul,
    In its mournful sighs !

O happy beam ! how canst thou prove
    That bright love of thine ?
In thy light is the proof of thy love,
    Thou hast but to shine !

How its love can the wind reveal?

Unwelcome its sigh;

Mute—mute to its rose let it steal—

Its proof is—to die!" *

* Reprinted from "The Last Days of Pompeii," by permission of Messrs George Routledge & Sons.

A VALENTINE.

LORD MACAULAY.

HAIL, day of music, day of love,
  On earth below, in air above.
  In air the turtle fondly moans,
The linnet pipes in joyous tones ;
On earth the postman toils along,
Bent double by huge bales of song,
Where, rich with many a gorgeous dye,
Blazes all Cupid's heraldry—
Myrtles and roses, doves and sparrows,
Love-knots and altars, lamps and arrows.
What nymph without wild hopes and fears
The double rap this morning hears?
Unnumbered lasses, young and fair,
From Bethnal Green to Belgrave Square,

With cheeks high flushed, and hearts loud beating,
Await the tender annual greeting.
The loveliest lass of all is mine—
Good-morrow to my Valentine!
Good-morrow, gentle child! and then
Again good-morrow, and again,
Good-morrow following still good-morrow,
Without one cloud of strife or sorrow.
And when the god to whom we pay
In jest our homages to-day
Shall come to claim, no more in jest,
His rightful empire o'er thy breast,
Benignant may his aspect be,
His yoke the truest liberty:
And if a tear his power confess,
Be it a tear of happiness.
It shall be so.   The Muse displays
The future to her votary's gaze;
Prophetic rage my bosom swells—
I taste the cake—I hear the bells!
From Conduit Street the close array
Of chariots barricades the way

To where I see, with outstretched hand,
Majestic, thy great kinsman stand,
And half unbend his brow of pride,
As welcoming so fair a bride.
Gay favours, thick as flakes of snow,
Brighten St George's portico :
Within I see the chancel's pale,
The orange flowers, the Brussels veil,
The page on which those fingers white,
Still trembling from the awful rite,
For the last time shall faintly trace
The name of Stanhope's noble race.
I see kind faces round thee pressing,
I hear kind voices whisper blessing ;
And with those voices mingles mine—
All good attend my Valentine !

LOVE'S REASONING.

CHARLES MACKAY.

HAT is the meaning of thy song,
    That rings so clear and loud ;
    Thou nightingale, amid the copse—
Thou lark above the cloud ?
What says thy song, thou joyous thrush
    Up in the walnut-tree ?—
" I love my love, because I know
    My love loves me."

What is the meaning of thy thought,
    O maiden fair and young ?
There is such pleasure in thine eyes,
    Such music on thy tongue ;

There is such glory in thy face,
    What can the meaning be?
"I love my love, because I know
    My love loves me!"

TO A FORGET-ME-NOT.

[*From the "Bon Gaultier Ballads."*]

THEODORE MARTIN.

WEET flower, that with thy soft blue eye
    Didst once look up in shady spot,
To whisper to the passer-by
Those tender words—Forget-me-not!

Though withered now, thou art to me
    The minister of gentle thought,—
And I could weep to gaze on thee,
    Love's faded pledge—Forget-me-not.

Thou speak'st of hours when I was young,
   And happiness arose unsought,
When she, the whispering woods among,
   Gave me thy bloom—Forget-me-not!

That rapturous hour with that dear maid
   From memory's page no time shall blot,
When, yielding to my kiss, she said,
   "O Theodore—Forget me not!"

Alas! for love, alas! for truth,
   Alas! for man's uncertain lot!
Alas! for all the hopes of youth,
   That fade like thee—Forget-me-not!

Alas! for that one image fair,
   With all my brightest dreams inwrought,
That walks beside me everywhere,
   Still whispering—Forget me not!

O Memory! thou art but a sigh
   For friendships dead and loves forgot;

And many a cold and altered eye,
   That once did say—Forget me not!

And I must bow me to thy laws,
   For—odd although it may be thought—
I can't tell who the deuce it was
   That gave me this Forget-me-not.

MADAME LA MARQUISE.

OWEN MEREDITH.

THE folds of her wine-dark violet dress
  Glow over the sofa, fall on fall,
As she sits in the air of her loveliness,
With a smile for each and for all.

Half of her exquisite face in the shade
  Which o'er it the screen in her soft hand flings;
Through the gloom glows her hair in its odorous braid;
  In the firelight are sparkling her rings.

As she leans,—the slow smile half shut up in her eyes
  Beams the sleepy, long, silk-soft lashes beneath:
Through her crimson lips, stirred by her faint replies,
  Breaks one gleam of her pearl-white teeth.

As she leans,—where your eye, by her beauty subdued,
  Droops—from under warm fringes of broidery white,
The slightest of feet, silken slippered, protrude
  For one moment, then slip out of sight.

As I bend o'er her bosom to tell her the news,
  The faint scent of her hair, the approach of her cheek,
The vague warmth of her breath, all my senses suffuse
  With HERSELF; and I tremble to speak.

So she sits in the curtained luxurious light
  Of that room with its porcelain, and pictures, and
    flowers,
When the dark day's half done, and the snow flutters
    white
  Past the windows in feathery showers.

All without is so cold,—'neath the low, leaden sky!
  Down the bald empty street, like a ghost, the
    gendarme
Stalks surly; a distant carriage hums by;—
  All within is so bright and so warm!

But she drives after noon;—then's the time to behold
    her,
  With her fair face, half hid, like a ripe peeping rose,
'Neath the veil,—o'er the velvets and furs which en-
    fold her,—
  Leaning back with a queenly repose.

As she glides up the sunlight, you'd say she was
    made
  To loll back in a carriage all day with a smile;
And at dusk, on a sofa, to lean in the shade
  Of soft lamps, and be wooed for a while.

Could we find out her heart through that velvet and
    lace!
  Can it beat without ruffling her sumptuous dress?
She will show us her shoulder, her bosom, her face;
  But what the heart's like, we must guess.

With live women and men to be found in the world—
  (Live with sorrow and sin—live with pain and with
    passion)—

Who could live with a doll, though its locks should
      be curled,
And its petticoats trimmed in the fashion?

'Tis so fair! Would my bite, if I bit it, draw blood?
  Will it cry if I hurt it? or scold if I kiss?
Is it made, with its beauty, of wax or of wood?
  . . . Is it worth while to guess at all this?

THE CHESSBOARD.

Owen Meredith.

DEAR little fool! do you remember,
  Ere we were grown so sadly wise,
    Those evenings in the bleak December,
Curtained warm from the snowy weather,
When you and I played chess together,
Checkmated by each other's eyes?
Ah! still I see your warm white hand
    Hovering o'er queen and knight;
Brave pawns in valiant battle stand;
The double castles guard the wings;
The bishop, bent on distant things,
    Moves, sidling, through the fight.
Our fingers touch; our glances meet,
And falter; falls your golden hair

Against my cheek ; your bosom sweet
Is heaving.   Down the field, your queen
Rides slow her soldiery all between,
    And checks me, unaware.
Ah me ! the little battle's done,
Disperst is all its chivalry.
Full many a move, since then, have we
'Mid life's perplexing chequers made,
And many a game with Fortune played,—
    What is it we have won?
This, this at least—if this alone ;—
That never, never, never more,
As in those old still nights of yore
(Ere we were grown so sadly wise),
Can you and I shut out the skies,
Shut out the world, and wintry weather,
And, eyes exchanging warmth with eyes,
Play chess, as then we played, together !

Owen Meredith.

SINCE we parted yester eve,
   I do love thee, love, believe
   Twelve times dearer, twelve hours longer,
One dream deeper, one night stronger,
One sun surer,—thus much more
Than I loved thee, love, before.

THE TIME I'VE LOST IN WOOING.

THOMAS MOORE.

THE time I've lost in wooing,
  In watching and pursuing
    The light that lies
    In Woman's eyes,
Has been my heart's undoing.
Though Wisdom oft has sought me,
I scorned the lore she brought me,
    My only books
    Were Woman's looks,
And folly's all they taught me.

Her smiles when Beauty granted,
I hung with gaze enchanted,

Like him, the sprite,

Whom maids by night

Oft meet in glen that's haunted.

Like him, too, Beauty won me

But while her eyes were on me ;

If once their ray

Was turned away,

Oh, winds could not outrun me !

And are those follies going ?

And is my proud heart growing

Too cold or wise

For brilliant eyes

Again to set it glowing ?

No,—vain, alas ! th' endeavour

From bonds so sweet to sever ;

Poor Wisdom's chance

Against a glance

Is now as weak as ever.

LOVE AND REASON.

THOMAS MOORE.

"SHE has beauty, but still you must keep your
    heart cool;
    She has wit, but you mustn't be caught so:"
Thus Reason advises, but Reason's a fool,
    And 'tis not the first time I have thought so,
        Dear Fanny,
'Tis not the first time I have thought so.

"She is lovely; then love her, nor let the bliss fly;
    'Tis the charm of youth's vanishing season:"
Thus Love has advised me, and who will deny
    That Love reasons much better than Reason,
        Dear Fanny?
Love reasons much better than Reason.

LOVE AND FRIENDSHIP.

Thomas Moore.

 TEMPLE to Friendship," said Laura, en-
    chanted,
    "I 'll build in this garden,—the thought is
    divine!"
Her temple was built, and she now only wanted
    An image of Friendship to place on the shrine.
She flew to a sculptor, who set down before her
    A Friendship, the fairest his art could invent;
But so cold and so dull, that the youthful adorer
    Saw plainly this was not the idol she meant.

"Oh, never," she cried, "could I think of enshrining
    An image whose looks are so joyless and dim;
But yon little god, upon roses reclining,
    We 'll make, if you please, sir, a Friendship of him."

R

So the bargain was struck : with the little god laden
  She joyfully flew to her shrine in the grove :
" Farewell," said the sculptor, " you 're not the first
    maiden
  Who came but for Friendship and took away Love."

THE CONTRAST.

CAPTAIN C. MORRIS.

IN London I never know what I 'd be at,
Enraptured with this, and enchanted with that;
I 'm wild with the sweets of variety's plan,
And life seems a blessing too happy for man.

But the country, Lord help me! sets all matters right,
So calm and composing from morning to night;
Oh, it settles the spirits when nothing is seen
But an ass on a common, a goose on a green!

In town, if it rain, why it damps not our hope,
The eye has her choice, and the fancy her scope;
What harm though it pour whole nights or whole days?
It spoils not our prospects, or stops not our ways.

In the country, what bliss, when it rains in the fields,
To live on the transports that shuttlecock yields ;
Or go crawling from window to window, to see
A pig on a dunghill or crow on a tree.

In town, we 've no use for the skies overhead,
For when the sun rises then we go to bed ;
And as to that old-fashioned virgin the moon,
She shines out of season, like satin in June.

In the country, these planets delightfully glare,
Just to show us the object we want isn't there ;
Oh, how cheering and gay, when their beauties arise,
To sit and gaze round with the tears in one's eyes !

But-'tis in the country alone we can find
That happy resource, that relief of the mind,
When, drove to despair, our last efforts we make,
And drag the old fish-pond, for novelty's sake :

Indeed I must own, 'tis a pleasure complete
To see ladies well draggled and wet in their feet;
But what is all that to the transport we feel
When we capture, in triumph, two toads and an eel?

I have heard though, that love in a cottage is sweet,
When two hearts in one link of soft sympathy meet;
That's to come—for as yet I, alas! am a swain,
Who require, I own it, more links to my chain.

In the country, if Cupid should find a man out,
The poor tortured victim mopes hopeless about;
But in London, thank Heaven! our peace is secure,
Where for one eye to kill, there's a thousand to cure.

In town let me live then, in town let me die,
For in truth I can't relish the country, not I.
If one must have a villa in summer to dwell,
Oh, give me the sweet shady side of Pall Mall!

LOVE AND FRIENDSHIP.

A CONCEIT.

SIR J. NOËL PATON.

SWEET! in the flowery garland of our love,
    Where fancy, folly, frenzy, interwove
    Our diverse destinies, not all unkind,
A secret strand of purest gold entwined.

While bloomed the magic flowers, we scarcely knew
The gold was there.   But now their petals strew
Life's pathway; and instead, with scarce a sigh,
We see the cold but fadeless circlet lie.

With scarce a sigh!—And yet the flowers were fair,
Fed by youth's dew and love's enchanted air;

Ay ! fair as youth and love ; but doomed, alas !
Like these and all things beautiful, to pass.

But this bright thread of unadulterate ore—
Friendship—will last though love exist no more ;
And though it lack the fragrance of the wreath,—
Unlike the flowers, it hides no thorn beneath.

Thomas L. Peacock.

I PLAYED with you, 'mid cowslips blowing,
  When I was six and you were four;
When garlands weaving, flower-balls throwing,
  Were pleasures soon to please no more.
Through groves and meads, o'er grass and heather,
  With little playmates, to and fro,
We wandered hand in hand together,—
  But that was sixty years ago.

You grew a lovely roseate maiden,
  And still our early love was strong;
Still with no care our days were laden,
  They glided joyously along;

And I did love you very dearly—
  How dearly, words want power to show;
I thought your heart was touched as nearly,—
  But that was fifty years ago.

Then other lovers came around you,
  Your beauty grew from year to year,
And many a splendid circle found you
  The centre of its glittering sphere.
I saw you then, first vows forsaking,
  On rank and wealth your hand bestow;
Oh, then I thought my heart was breaking,—
  But that was forty years ago.

And I lived on, to wed another:
  No cause she gave me to repine;
And when I heard you were a mother,
  I did not wish the children mine.
My own young flock, in fair progression,
  Made up a pleasant Christmas row:
My joy in them was past expression,—
  But that was thirty years ago.

You grew a matron plump and comely,
　　You dwelt in fashion's brightest blaze;
My earthly lot was far more homely,
　　But I too had my festal days.
No merrier eyes have ever glistened
　　Around the hearthstone's wintry glow,
Than when my youngest child was christened,—
　　But that was twenty years ago.

Time past; my eldest girl was married,
　　And I am now a grandsire grey;
One pet of four years old I 've carried
　　Among the wild-flowered meads to play.
In our old fields of childish pleasure,
　　Where now, as then, the cowslips blow,
She fills her basket's ample measure,—
　　And that is not ten years ago.

But though first love's impassioned blindness
　　Has passed away in colder light,
I still have thought of you with kindness,
　　And shall do, till our last good-night.

The ever-rolling silent hours
  Will bring a time we shall not know,
When our young days of gathering flowers
  Will be an hundred years ago.

OUR BALL.

W. M. PRAED.

YOU 'LL come to our ball :—since we parted
   I 've thought of you more than I 'll say ;
   Indeed, I was half broken-hearted
For a week, when they took you away.
Fond fancy brought back to my slumbers
   Our walks on the Ness and the Den,
And echoed the musical numbers
   Which you used to sing to me then.
I know the romance, now 'tis over,
   'Twere idle, or worse, to recall ;
I know you 're a terrible rover ;
   But, Clarence, you 'll come to our ball.

It's only a year since at college
    You put on your cap and your gown;
But, Clarence, you've grown out of knowledge,
    And changed from the spur to the crown:
The voice, that was best when it faltered,
    Is firmer and fuller in tone,
And the smile, that should never have altered,
    Dear Clarence, it is not your own.
Your cravat was badly selected,
    Your coat don't become you at all;
And why is your hair so neglected?
    You must have it curled for our ball.

I've often been out upon Haldon
    To look for a covey with Pup;
I've often been over to Shaldon
    Too see how your boat is laid up:
In spite of the terrors of Aunty
    I've ridden the filly you broke;
And I've studied your sweet little Dante
    In the shade of your favourite oak.

When I sat in July to Sir Lawrence,
　　I sat in your love of a shawl;
And I'll wear what you brought me from Florence,
　　Perhaps, if you'll come to our ball.

You'll find us all changed since you vanished:
　　We've set up a National school,
And waltzing is utterly banished,
　　And Ellen has married a fool.
The Major is going to travel;
　　Miss Hyacinth threatens a rout;
The walk is laid down with fresh gravel,
　　And papa is laid up with the gout.
And Jane has gone on with her easels;
　　And Anne has gone off with Sir Paul;
And Fanny is sick with the measles,—
　　And I'll tell you the rest at the ball.

You'll meet all your beauties: the Lily,
　　And the Fairy of Willowbrook Farm,
And Lucy, who made me so silly
　　At Dawlish, by taking your arm,

Miss Manners, who always abused you
   For talking so much about hock ;
And her sister, who often amused you
   By raving of rebels and Rock ;
And something which surely would answer,
   An heiress quite fresh from Bengal ;
So, though you were seldom a dancer,
   You 'll dance, just for once, at our ball.

But out on the world ! from the flowers,
   It shuts out the sunshine of truth ;
It blights the green leaves in our bowers,
   It makes an old age of our youth ;
And the flow of our feeling, once in it,
   Like a streamlet beginning to freeze,
Though it cannot turn ice in a minute,
   Grows harder by sudden degrees.
Time treads o'er the graves of affection ;
   Sweet honey is turned into gall :
Perhaps you have no recollection
   That ever you danced at our ball :

You once could be pleased with our ballads;—
　　To-day you have critical ears;
You once could be charmed with our salads;—
　　Alas! you 've been dining with peers.
You trifled and flirted with many;—
　　You 've forgotten the when and the how:
There was one you liked better than any,—
　　Perhaps you 've forgotten her now.
But of those you remember most newly,
　　Of those who delight and enthrall,
None love you a quarter so truly
　　As some you will find at our ball.

They tell me you 've many who flatter,
　　Because of your wit and your song;
They tell me—and what does it matter?—
　　You like to be praised by the throng:
They tell me you 're shadowed with laurel;
　　They tell me you 're loved by a Blue;
They tell me you 're sadly immoral:—
　　Dear Clarence, that cannot be true!

But to me you are still what I found you,
  Before you grew clever and tall;
And you'll think of the spell that once bound you;
  And you'll come—won't you come?—to our ball.

TO HELEN.

W. M. PRAED.

IF, wandering in a wizard's car
    Through yon blue ether, I were able
  To fashion of a little star
A taper for my Helen's table ;—

" What then ?" she asks me with a laugh ;—
  Why, then, with all heaven's lustre glowing,
It would not gild her path with half
  The light her love o'er mine is throwing !

THE BELLE OF THE BALL-ROOM.

W. M. PRAED.

EARS—years ago, ere yet my dreams
  Had been of being wise or witty,—
  Ere I had done with writing themes,
 Or yawned o'er this infernal Chitty ;—
Years—years ago,—while all my joy
 Was in my fowling-piece and filly,—
In short, while I was yet a boy,
 I fell in love with Laura Lily.

I saw her at the county ball :
 There, when the sounds of flute and fiddle
Gave signal sweet in that old hall
 Of hands across and down the middle,

Hers was the subtlest spell by far
    Of all that set young hearts romancing;
She was our queen, our rose, our star;
    And then she danced—O Heaven, her dancing!

Dark was her hair, her hand was white;
    Her voice was exquisitely tender;
Her eyes were full of liquid light;
    I never saw a waist so slender!
Her every look, her every smile,
    Shot right and left a score of arrows;
I thought 'twas Venus from her isle,
    And wondered where she'd left her sparrows.

She talked,—of politics or prayers,—
    Or Southey's prose, or Wordsworth's sonnets,—
Of danglers,—or of dancing bears,—
    Of battles,—or the last new bonnets.
By candlelight, at twelve o'clock,
    To me it mattered not a tittle;
If those bright lips had quoted Locke,
    I might have thought they murmured Little.

Through sunny May, through sultry June,
   I loved her with a love eternal ;
I spoke her praises to the moon,
   I wrote them to the *Sunday Journal.*
My mother laughed ; I soon found out
   That ancient ladies have no feeling :
My father frowned ; but how should gout
   See any happiness in kneeling ?

She was the daughter of a Dean,
   Rich, fat, and rather apoplectic ;
She had one brother, just thirteen,
   Whose colour was extremely hectic ;
Her grandmother for many a year
   Had fed the parish with her bounty ;
Her second cousin was a peer,
   And Lord-Lieutenant of the county.

But titles, and the three per cents.,
   And mortgages, and great relations,
And India bonds, and tithes, and rents,
   Oh, what are they to love's sensations ?

Black eyes, fair forehead, clustering locks—
　　Such wealth, such honours, Cupid chooses ;
He cares as little for the Stocks
　　As Baron Rothschild for the Muses.

She sketched ; the vale, the wood, the beach,
　　Grew lovelier from her pencil's shading :
She botanised ; I envied each
　　Young blossom in her boudoir fading :
She warbled Handel ; it was grand ;
　　She made the Catalani jealous :
She touched the organ ; I could stand
　　For hours and hours to blow the bellows.

She kept an album, too, at home,
　　Well filled with all an album's glories ;
Paintings of butterflies and Rome,
　　Patterns for trimmings, Persian stories,
Soft songs to Julia's cockatoo,
　　Fierce odes to Famine and to Slaughter,
And autographs of Prince Leboo,
　　And recipes for elder-water.

And she was flattered, worshipped, bored ;
　Her steps were watched, her dress was noted ;
Her poodle dog was quite adored,
　Her sayings were extremely quoted ;
She laughed, and every heart was glad,
　As if the taxes were abolished ;
She frowned, and every look was sad,
　As if the opera were demolished.

She smiled on many, just for fun,—
　I knew that there was nothing in it ;
I was the first—the only one
　Her heart had thought of for a minute.
I knew it, for she told me so,
　In phrase which was divinely moulded ;
She wrote a charming hand,—and oh !
　How sweetly all her notes were folded !

Our love was like most other loves ;—
　A little glow, a little shiver,
A rosebud, and a pair of gloves,
　And " Fly not yet "—upon the river ;

Some jealousy of some one's heir,
   Some hopes of dying broken-hearted,
A miniature, a lock of hair,
   The usual vows,—and then we parted.

We parted; months and years rolled by;
   We met again four summers after:
Our parting was all sob and sigh;
   Our meeting was all mirth and laughter:
For in my heart's most secret cell
   There had been many other lodgers;
And she was not the ball-room's belle,
   But only—Mrs Something Rogers!

A LETTER OF ADVICE.

W. M. PRAED.

YOU tell me you're promised a lover,
My own Araminta, next week;
Why cannot my fancy discover
The hue of his coat and his cheek?
Alas! if he look like another,
A vicar, a banker, a beau,
Be deaf to your father and mother,
My own Araminta, say "No!"

Miss Lane, at her Temple of Fashion,
Taught us both how to sing and to speak,
And we loved one another with passion
Before we had been there a week:

You gave me a ring for a token ;
   I wear it wherever I go :
I gave you a chain,—is it broken ?
   My own Araminta, say " No ! "

O think of our favourite cottage,
   And think of our dear " Lalla Rookh ! "
How we shared with the milkmaids their pottage,
   And drank of the stream from the brook ;
How fondly our loving lips faltered,
   " What further can grandeur bestow ? "
My heart is the same ;—is yours altered ?
   My own Araminta, say " No ! "

Remember the thrilling romances
   We read on the bank in the glen ;
Remember the suitors our fancies
   Would picture for both of us then.
They wore the red cross on their shoulder,
   They had vanquished and pardoned their foe ;—
Sweet friend, are you wiser or colder ?
   My own Araminta, say " No ! "

You know, when Lord Rigmarole's carriage
  Drove off with your cousin Justine,
You wept, dearest girl, at the marriage,
  And whispered "How base she has been!"
You said you were sure it would kill you
  If ever your husband looked so;
And you will not apostatise,—will you?
  My own Araminta, say "No!"

When I heard I was going abroad, love,
  I thought I was going to die;
We walked arm-in-arm to the road, love,
  We looked arm-in-arm to the sky;
And I said, "When a foreign postilion
  Has hurried me off to the Po,
Forget not Medora Trevilian:
  My own Araminta, say 'No!'"

We parted! but sympathy's fetters
  Reach far over valley and hill;
I muse o'er your exquisite letters,
  And feel that your heart is mine still;

And he who would share it with me, love,—
The richest of treasures below,—
If he's not what Orlando should be, love,
My own Araminta, say " No ! "

If he wears a top-boot in his wooing,
If he comes to you riding a cob,
If he talks of his baking or brewing,
If he puts up his feet on the hob,
If he ever drinks port after dinner,
If his brow or his breeding is low,
If he calls himself " Thompson " or Skinner,"
My own Araminta, say " No ! "

If he studies the news in the papers
While you are preparing the tea,
If he talks of the damps or the vapours
While moonlight lies soft on the sea,
If he's sleepy while you are capricious,
If he has not a musical " Oh ! "
If he does not call Werther delicious,
My own Araminta, say " No ! "

If he ever sets foot in the City
    Among the stockbrokers and Jews,
If he has not a heart full of pity,
    If he don't stand six feet in his shoes,
If his lips are not redder than roses,
    If his hands are not whiter than snow,
If he has not the model of noses,—
    My own Araminta, say "No!"

If he speaks of a tax or a duty,
    If he does not look grand on his knees,
If he's blind to a landscape of beauty,
    Hills, valleys, rocks, waters, and trees,
If he dotes not on desolate towers,
    If he likes not to hear the blast blow,
If he knows not the language of flowers,—
    My own Araminta, say "No!"

He must walk—like a god of old story
    Come down from the home of his rest;
He must smile—like the sun in his glory
    On the buds he loves ever the best;

And oh ! from its ivory portal
  Like music his soft speech must flow !—
If he speak, smile, or walk like a mortal,
  My own Araminta, say " No ! "

Don't listen to tales of his bounty,
  Don't hear what they say of his birth,
Don't look at his seat in the county,
  Don't calculate what he is worth ;
But give him a theme to write verse on,
  And see if he turns out his toe ;
If he 's only an excellent person,—
  My own Araminta, say " No ! "

THE PACE THAT KILLS.

W. J. PROWSE.

THE gallop of life was once exciting,
    Madly we dashed over pleasant plains;
    And the joy, like the joy of a brave man fighting,
Poured in a flood through our eager veins.
Hot youth is the time for the splendid ardour
    That stings and startles, that throbs and thrills;
And ever we pressed our horses harder,
    Galloping on at the pace that kills!

So rapid the pace, so keen the pleasure,
    Scarcely we paused to glance aside,
As we mocked the dullards who watched at leisure
    The frantic race that we chose to ride.

Yes, youth is the time when a master-passion,
　Or love or ambition, our nature fills ;
And each of us rode in a different fashion—
　All of us rode at the pace that kills !

And vainly, O friends ! ye strive to bind us ;
　Flippantly, gaily, we answer you :
"Should ATRA CURA jump up behind us,
　Strong are our steeds, and can carry two !"
But we find the road, so smooth at morning,
　Rugged at night 'mid the lonely hills ;
And all too late we recall the warning,
　Weary at last of the pace that kills !

　　.　　　.　　　.　　　.　　　.　　　.

The gallop of life was just beginning ;
　Strength we wasted in efforts vain ;
And now when the prizes are worth the winning,
　We 've scarcely the spirit to ride again !
The spirit, forsooth !　'Tis our strength has failed us,
　And sadly we ask, as we count our ills,
"What pitiful, pestilent folly ailed us?
　Why did we ride at the pace that kills ?"

MY LOST OLD AGE.

BY A YOUNG INVALID.

W. J. PROWSE.

'M only nine-and-twenty yet,
 Though young experience makes me sage ;
 So, how on earth can *I* forget
The memory of my lost old age ?
Of manhood's prime let others boast ;
 It comes too late, or goes too soon :
At times the life I envy most
 Is that of slippered pantaloon !

In days of old—a twelvemonth back !—
 I laughed, and quaffed, and chaffed my fill ;

T

And now, a broken-winded hack,
  I 'm weak and worn, and faint and ill.

Life's opening chapter pleased me well ;
  Too hurriedly I turned the page ;
I spoiled the volume—— Who can tell
  What *might* have been my lost old age ?

I lived my life ; I had my day ;
  And now I feel it more and more :
The game I have no strength to play
  Seems better than it seemed of yore.
I watch the sport with earnest eyes,
  That gleam with joy before it ends ;
For plainly I can hear the cries
  That hail the triumph of my friends.

We work so hard, we age so soon,
  We live so swiftly, one and all,
That ere our day be fairly noon
  The shadows eastward seem to fall.

Some tender light may gild them yet;
As yet, it's not so *very* cold;
And, on the whole, I won't regret
My slender chance of growing old!

"NO, THANK YOU, JOHN!

CHRISTINA ROSSETTI.

I NEVER said I loved you, John:
　　Why will you tease me day by day,
　And wax a weariness to think upon,
　　With always " Do" and " Pray"?

You know I never loved you, John;
　　No fault of mine made me your toast:
　Why will you haunt me with a face so wan
　　As shows an hour-old ghost?

I daresay Meg or Moll would take
　　Pity upon you, if you'd ask:
　And pray don't remain single for my sake,
　　Who can't perform that task.

I have no heart ?—Perhaps I have not ;
  But then you 're mad to take offence
That I don't give you what I have not got :
  Use your own common sense.

Let bygones be bygones :
  Don't call me false, who owned not to be true :
I 'd rather answer " No " to fifty Johns
  Than answer " Yes " to you.

Let 's mar our pleasant days no more,
  Song-birds of passage, days of youth :
Catch at to-day, forget the days before
  I 'll wink at your untruth.

Let us strike hands as hearty friends,—
  No more, no less ; and friendship 's good :
Only don't keep in view ulterior ends,
  And points not understood

In open treaty.   Rise above
   Quibbles and shuffling off and on :
Here 's friendship for you if you like ; but love,—
   No, thank you, John !

A MATCH WITH THE MOON.

DANTE G. ROSSETTI.

WEARY already, weary miles to-night
   I walked for bed : and so, to get some ease,
   I dogged the flying moon with similes.
And like a wisp she doubled on my sight
In ponds ; and caught in tree-tops like a kite ;
And in a globe of film all vapourish
Swam full-faced like a silly silver fish ;—
Last, like a bubble shot the welkin's height,
Where my road turned, and got behind me, and sent
My wizened shadow craning round at me,
And jeered, "So, step the measure,—one, two, three !"
And if I faced on her, looked innocent.
But just at parting, half-way down a dell,
She kissed me for good-night.   So you 'll not tell.

AT THE OPERA—"FAUST."

[*Extract.*]

WILLIAM SAWYER.

T came with the curtain's rising,
  That face of a faultless mould,
And the amber drapery glistened
With the lustre of woven gold.
I could hear a silken rustle,
  And the air had fragrant grown,
But the scene from my sight had faded,
  And I looked on that face alone.

In the midst of the grand exotics
  That blossom the season through,
It is there, a rose of the garden
  Fresh from the winds and the dew ;—

Fresh as a face that follows
  The hounds up a rimy hill,
With hair blown back by the breezes
  That seem to live in it still.

So fresh and rosy and dimpled—
  But, oh ! what a soul there lies,
Melting to liquid agate
  Those womanly tender eyes !
How it quickens under the music,
  As if at a breath divine,
And the ripening lips disparted
  Drink in the sound like wine ! . . .

Till the music surges and ceases,
  As the sea when the wind is spent,
And the blue of heaven brightens
  Through cloudy fissure and rent.
It ceases,—and all is over,
  The box is empty and cold,
And the amber drapery deadens
  To satin that has been gold.

WILLIAM SAWYER.

SUNNY breadth of roses,
    Roses white and red,
    Rosy bud and rose leaf
From the blossom shed !
·Goes my darling flying
    All the garden through ;
Laughing she eludes me,
    Laughing I pursue.

Now to pluck the rosebud,
    Now to pluck the rose
(Hand a sweeter blossom),
    Stopping as she goes :

What but this contents her,
Laughing in her flight,
Pelting with the red rose,
Pelting with the white.

Roses round me flying,
Roses in my hair,
I to snatch them trying :
Darling, have a care !
Lips are so like flowers,
I might snatch at those,
Redder than the rose leaves,
Sweeter than the rose.

MY FAMILIAR.

J GODFREY SAXE.

GAIN I hear that creaking step !—
He's rapping at the door !—
Too well I know the boding sound
That ushers in a bore.
I do not tremble when I meet
The stoutest of my foes,
But Heaven defend me from the friend
Who comes—but never goes !

He drops into my easy-chair,
And asks about the news ;
He peers into my manuscript,
And gives his candid views ;

He tells me where he likes the line,
　And where he 's forced to grieve;
He takes the strangest liberties,—
　But never takes his leave!

He reads my daily paper through
　Before I 've seen a word;
He scans the lyric (that I wrote),
　And thinks it quite absurd;
He calmly smokes my last cigar,
　And coolly asks for more;
He opens everything he sees—
　Except the entry door!

He talks about his fragile health,
　And tells me of the pains;
He suffers from a score of ills
　Of which he ne'er complains;
And how he struggled once with death
　To keep the fiend at bay;
On themes like those away he goes—
　But never goes away!

He tells me of the carping words
　　Some shallow critic wrote;
And every precious paragraph
　　Familiarly can quote;
He thinks the writer did me wrong;
　　He 'd like to run him through!
He says a thousand pleasant things—
　　But never says " Adieu!"

Whene'er he comes—that dreadful man—
　　Disguise it as I may,
I know that, like an autumn rain,
　　He 'll last throughout the day.
In vain I speak of urgent tasks;
　　In vain I scowl and pout;
A frown is no extinguisher—
　　It does not put him out!

I mean to take the knocker off,
　　Put crape upon the door,
Or hint to John that I am gone
　　To stay a month or more.

I do not tremble when I meet
　The stoutest of my foes,
But Heaven defend me from the friend
　Who never, never goes !

A U G U S T A.

J. GODFREY SAXE.

"HANDSOME and haughty ! "—a comment that came
  From lips which were never accustomed to malice ;
A girl with a presence superb as her name,
And charmingly fitted for love—in a palace !
And oft I have wished,—for in musing alone
One's fancy is apt to be very erratic,—
That the lady might wear—No ! I never will own
A thought so decidedly undemocratic !
But *if* 'twere a *coronet*—this I 'll aver,
No duchess on earth could more gracefully wear it ;
And even a democrat—thinking of *her*—
Might surely be pardoned for wishing to share it.

"DO YOU THINK HE IS MARRIED?"

J. GODFREY SAXE.

MADAM, you are very pressing,
  And I can't decline the task ;
With the slightest gift of guessing,
You would scarcely need to ask !

Don't you see a hint of marriage
  In his sober-sided face,
In his rather careless carriage,
  And extremely rapid pace ?

If he 's not committed treason,
  Or some wicked action done,
Can you see the faintest reason
  Why a bachelor should run ?

U

Why should he be in a flurry?
But a loving wife to greet
Is a circumstance to hurry
The most dignified of feet !

When afar the man has spied her,
If the grateful, happy elf
Does not haste to be beside her,
He must be beside himself!

It is but a trifle, maybe,—
But observe his practised tone
When he calms your stormy baby,
Just as if it were his own.

Do you think a certain meekness
You have mentioned in his looks,
Is a chronic optic weakness
That has come of reading books?

Did you ever see his vision
  Peering underneath a hood,
Save enough for recognition,
  As a civil person should?

Could a Capuchin be colder
  When he glances, as he must,
At a finely rounded shoulder
  Or a proudly swelling bust?

Madam!—think of every feature,
  Then deny it if you can,—
He 's a fond, connubial creature,
  And a *very* married man!

LOVE'S PHILOSOPHY.

Percy Bysshe Shelley.

THE fountains mingle with the river,
   And the rivers with the ocean,
   The winds of heaven mix for ever
With a sweet emotion!
Nothing in the world is single;
   All things, by a law divine,
In one another's being mingle—
Why not I with thine?

See, the mountains kiss high heaven,
   And the waves clasp one another;
No sister flower would be forgiven
If it disdained its brother:

And the sunlight clasps the earth,
   And the moonbeams kiss the sea :
What are all these kissings worth,
   If thou kiss not me?

TO E——— V———.

PERCY BYSSHE SHELLEY.

MADONNA ! wherefore hast thou sent to me
  Sweet-basil and mignonette,
Embleming love and health, which never
   yet
  In the same wreath might be ?
  Alas ! and they are wet !
Is it with thy kisses or thy tears ?
  For never rain or dew
  Such fragrance drew
From plant or flower :—the very doubt endears
  My sadness ever new,
The sighs I breathe, the tears I shed for thee.

SONG TO FANNY.

HORACE SMITH.

NATURE! thy fair and smiling face
   Has now a double power to bless,
   For 'tis the glass in which I trace
My absent Fanny's loveliness.

Her heavenly eyes above me shine,
   The rose reflects her modest blush,
She breathes in every eglantine,
   She sings in every warbling thrush.

That *her* dear form alone I see
   Need not excite surprise in any,
For Fanny 's all the world to me,
   And all the world to me is Fanny.

TO LADY ANNE HAMILTON.

Hon. William R. Spencer.

TOO late I stayed ! forgive the crime,—
Unheeded flew the hours ;
How noiseless falls the foot of Time
That only treads on flowers !

What eye with clear account remarks
The ebbing of his glass,
When all its sands are diamond sparks,
That dazzle as they pass?

Ah ! who to sober measurement
Time's happy swiftness brings,
When birds of paradise have lent
Their plumage for his wings ?

EPITAPH UPON THE YEAR 1806.

Hon. William R. Spencer.

'TIS gone, with its thorns and its roses,
    With the dust of dead ages to mix;
  Time's charnel for ever encloses
The year Eighteen hundred and six!

Though many may question thy merit,
  I duly thy dirge will perform,
Content, if thy heir but inherit
  Thy portion of sunshine and storm!

My blame and my blessing thou sharest,
  For black were thy moments in part,
But oh, thy fair days were the fairest
  That ever have shone on my heart.

If thine was a gloom the completest
    That death's darkest cypress could throw,
Thine, too, was a garland the sweetest
    That life in full blossom could show !

One hand gave the balmy corrector
    Of ills which the other had brewed ;
One draught of thy chalice of nectar
    All taste of thy bitters subdued.

'Tis gone, with its thorns and its roses !
    With mine, tears more precious will mix,
To hallow this midnight which closes
    The year Eighteen hundred and six.

WIFE, CHILDREN, AND FRIENDS.

Hon. William R. Spencer.

WHEN the black-lettered list to the gods was
presented
(The list of what Fate for each mortal
intends),
At the long string of ills a kind goddess relented,
And slipt in three blessings—wife, children, and
friends.

In vain surely Pluto maintained he was cheated,
For justice divine could not compass her ends;
The scheme of man's penance he swore was defeated,
For earth becomes heav'n with wife, children, and
friends.

If the stock of our bliss is in stranger hands vested,
　　The fund, ill-secured, oft in bankruptcy ends ;
But the heart issues bills which are never protested
　　When drawn on the firm of Wife, Children, and
　　　　Friends.

　　.　　　.　　　.　　　.　　　.　　　.　　　.

Let the breath of renown ever freshen and cherish
　　The laurel which o'er her dead favourite bends,
O'er me wave the willow, and long may it flourish,
　　Bedewed with the tears of wife, children, and friends.

Let us drink—for my song, growing graver and
　　　　graver,
　　To subjects too solemn insensibly tends ;
Let us drink—pledge me high ;—Love and Virtue
　　　　shall flavour
　　The glass which I fill to wife, children, and friends.

LITTLE GERTY.

FRANK STAINFORTH.

'VE a sweetheart blithe and gay,
  Fairer far than fabled fay,
    Light and airy.
She is bright and debonnaire,
Softly falls her golden hair;
I all other loves forswear:
    Little fairy.

Little Gerty swears she 's true,
Gives me kisses not a few;
    Do I doubt her?
Hearts are often bought and sold;
Is it glitter, is it gold?

Half my grief could not be told
Were I without her.

Gerty scolds me if I roam,
Wonders what I want from home,
With sly glances—
Looks that seem to me to say,
" I have waited all the day ;
You were very wrong to stray,
Naughty Francis."

If I whisper, " We must part,"
Gerty, sighing, breaks her heart ;
Awkward, very.
When I say that I 'll remain,
All her smiles return again,
Like warm sunshine after rain ;
We are merry.

If my sweetheart knows her mind,
Love is mad as well as blind.
Little Gerty

Says she means to marry me ;

She is only six, you see ;

I—alas, that it should be !—

Am two-and-thirty.*

* Reprinted, by permission, from *Cassell's Magazine.*

THE HUSBAND'S SONG.

CHARLES SWAIN.

RAINY and rough sets the day,—
　　There 's a heart beating for somebody ;
I must be up and away,—
Somebody 's anxious for somebody.
Thrice hath she been to the gate,—
　　Thrice hath she listened for somebody ;
'Midst the night, stormy and late,
　　Somebody 's waiting for somebody.

There 'll be a comforting fire,
　　There 'll be a welcome for somebody ;
One, in her neatest attire,
　　Will look at the table for somebody.

Though the stars fled from the west,
  There is a star yet for somebody,
Lighting the home he loves best,
  Warming the bosom of somebody.

There 'll be a coat o'er the chair,
  There will be slippers for somebody;
There 'll be a wife's tender care,—
  Love's fond embracement for somebody;
There 'll be the little one's charms,—
  Soon 'twill be wakened for somebody;
When I have both in my arms,
  Oh ! but how blest will be somebody

X

A MATCH.

ALGERNON CHARLES SWINBURNE.

IF love were what the rose is,
    And I were like the leaf,
    Our lives would grow together
In sad or singing weather,
Blown fields or flowerful closes,
    Green pleasure or grey grief;
If love were what the rose is,
    And I were like the leaf.

If I were what the words are,
    And love were like the tune,
With double sound and single
Delight our lips would mingle,

With kisses glad as birds are
    That get sweet rain at noon;
If I were what the words are,
    And love were like the tune.

If you were Life, my darling,
    And I your love were Death,
We'd shine and snow together
Ere March made sweet the weather
With daffodil and starling
    And hours of fruitful breath;
If you were Life, my darling,
    And I your love were Death.

If you were thrall to Sorrow,
    And I were page to Joy,
We'd play for lives and seasons
With loving looks and treasons,
And tears of night and morrow,
    And laughs of maid and boy;
If you were thrall to Sorrow,
    And I were page to Joy.

If you were April's lady,
　And I were lord in May,
We 'd throw with leaves for hours,
And draw for days with flowers,
Till day like night were shady,
　And night were bright like day;
If you were April's lady,
　And I were lord in May.

If you were queen of pleasure,
　And I were king of pain,
We 'd hunt down Love together,
Pluck out his flying feather,
And teach his feet a measure,
　And find his mouth a rein;
If you were queen of pleasure,
　And I were king of pain.

FÉLISE.

[*Extract.*]

Mais où sont les neiges d'antan?

ALGERNON CHARLES SWINBURNE.

HAT shall be said between us here,
  Among the downs, between the trees,
In fields that knew our feet last year,
In sight of quiet sands and seas,
This year, Félise?

Who knows what word were best to say?
  For last year's leaves lie dead and red
On this sweet day, in this green May,
  And barren corn makes bitter bread:
What shall be said?

Here, as last year, the fields begin,
    A fire of flowers and glowing grass ;—
The old fields we laughed and lingered in,
    Seeing each our souls in last year's glass,
    Félise, alas !

Shall we not laugh, shall we not weep ?
    Not we, though this be as it is ;
For love awake or love asleep
    Ends in a laugh, a dream, a kiss,
    A song like this.

I that have slept, awake, and you
    Sleep, who last year were well awake :
Though love do all that love can do,
    My love will never ache or break
    For your heart's sake.

The great sea, faultless as a flower,
    Throbs, trembling under beam and breeze,

And laughs with love of the amorous hour.
    I found you fairer once, Félise,
    Than flowers or seas.

We played at bondsman and at queen;
    But as the days change men change too;
I find the grey sea's notes of green,
    The green sea's fervent flakes of blue,
    More fair than you.

Your beauty is not over-fair
    Now in mine eyes, who am grown up wise;
The smell of flowers in all your hair
    Allures not now; no sigh replies
    If your heart sighs.

But you sigh seldom, you sleep sound;
    You find love's new name good enough:
Less sweet I find it than I found
    The sweetest name that ever love
    Grew weary of.

ALGERNON CHARLES SWINBURNE.

ON the greenest growth of the May-time,
   I rode where the woods were wet,
  Between the dawn and the day-time;
   The spring was glad that we met.

There was something the season wanted,
   Though the ways and the woods smelt sweet;
The breath at your lips that panted,
   The pulse of the grass at your feet.

You came, and the sun came after,
   And the green grew golden above;
And the May-flowers lightened with laughter,
   And the meadow-sweet shook with love.

Your feet in the full-grown grasses
　　Moved soft as a weak wind blows;
You passed me as April passes,
　　With face made out of a rose.

By the stream where the stems were slender,
　　Your light foot paused at the sedge;
It might be to watch the tender
　　Light leaves in the spring-time hedge,

On boughs that the sweet month blanches
　　With flowery frost of May;
It might be a bird in the branches,
　　It might be a thorn in the way.

I waited to watch you linger,
　　With foot drawn back from the dew,
Till a sunbeam straight like a finger
　　Struck sharp through the leaves at you.

And a bird overhead sang " Follow,"
　　And a bird to the right sang " Here ; "
And the arch of the leaves was hollow,
　　And the meaning of May was clear.

I saw where the sun's hand pointed,
　　I knew what the bird's note said ;
By the dawn and the dewfall anointed,
　　You were queen by the gold on your head.

As the glimpse of a burnt-out ember
　　Recalls a regret of the sun,
I remember, forget, and remember
　　What love saw done and undone.

I remember the way we parted,
　　The day and the way we met ;
You hoped we were both broken-hearted,
　　And knew we should both forget.

And May with her world in flower
   Seemed still to murmur and smile
As you murmured and smiled for an hour;
   I saw you twice at the stile.

A hand like a white-wood blossom
   You lifted, and waved, and passed,
With head hung down to the bosom,
   And pale, as it seemed, to the last.

And the best and the worst of this is,
   That neither is most to blame,
If you 've forgotten my kisses,
   And I 've forgotten your name.

L I L I A N.

Alfred Tennyson.

AIRY, fairy Lilian,
    Flitting, fairy Lilian,
      When I ask her if she love me,
Claps her tiny hands above me,
    Laughing all she can ;
She 'll not tell me if she love me,
    Cruel little Lilian.

    When my passion seeks
    Pleasance in love-sighs,
She, looking through and through me,
Thoroughly to undo me,
    Smiling, never speaks :

So innocent-arch, so cunning-simple,
From beneath her gathered wimple
   Glancing with black-beaded eyes,
Till the lightning laughters dimple
   The baby-roses in her cheeks;
   Then away she flies.

Prithee weep, May Lilian!
  Gaiety without eclipse
Wearieth me, May Lilian:
Through my very heart it thrilleth,
  When from crimson-threaded lips
Silver-treble laughter trilleth:
Prithee weep, May Lilian!

   Praying all I can,
If prayers will not hurt thee,
   Airy Lilian,
Like a rose-leaf I will crush thee,
   Fairy Lilian.

TO A COQUETTE.

Alfred Tennyson.

HE form, the form alone is eloquent !
    A nobler yearning never broke her rest
    Than but to dance and sing, be gaily drest,
And win all eyes with all accomplishment :
Yet in the waltzing circle as we went,
My fancy made me for a moment blest
To find my heart so near the beauteous breast
That once had power to rob it of content.
A moment came the tenderness of tears,
The phantom of a wish that once could move,
A ghost of passion that no smiles restore—
For ah ! the slight coquette, she cannot love,
And if you kissed her feet a thousand years,
She still would take the praise, and care no more.

UNDER THE CLIFFS.

[Extract.]

WALTER THORNBURY.

HE sails, now white as a swan's breast,
   Turned in a moment golden
The red-brown canvas, fluttering out,
  Was presently all folden.
The tide came rolling to our feet,
  With spreading frills of snow,
As on the sand, so brown and soft,
  We sat amid the glow.

Oh, all the hour-glass sands that Time
   Had spilt lay there around us!
Yet still forgetful of day's flight
  The mystic twilight found us.

As the large moon and smouldering globe
Of orange-fire rose slow,
And home we wandered to the town,
Love's ebb had turned to flow.

THE FALLING OF THE LEAVES.

[*Extract.*]

WALTER THORNBURY.

CLEAR, keen, and pure, the sunny air
  Is bright as summer's, and as fair;
  But many a branch is growing bare,
    And leaves are falling.
October skies are coldly blue,
The grass is silvery wet with dew,
And berries crimson to the view,
    While leaves are falling.
Thick webs wrap every hedge in grey,
Dull mists shroud up the dying day;
Black vapours bar the labourer's way,
    And leaves are falling.

Like ghosts, pale drifts of mournful light
Stretch in the west, and on the night
Look with sad faces, wan and white,
    While leaves are falling.

How many autumns I have known !
But each one finds me more alone ;
Now youth has left its royal throne,
    And leaves are falling.

Yet, Hope, wear still thy starry crown,
Point to far statues of renown,
And bid me trample sorrows down,
    Though leaves be falling.

KITTY OF COLERAINE.

UNKNOWN.

AS beautiful Kitty one morning was tripping
    With a pitcher of milk from the fair of
        Coleraine,
When she saw me she stumbled, the pitcher it tumbled,
    And all the sweet butter-milk watered the plain.

" Oh, what shall I do now ? 'twas looking at you now ;
    Sure, sure such a pitcher I 'll ne'er meet again ;
'Twas the pride of my dairy,—O Barney M'Leary,
    You 're sent as a plague to the girls of Coleraine."

I sat down beside her, and gently did chide her
    That such a misfortune should give her such pain ;

A kiss then I gave her,—before I did leave her
  She vowed for such pleasure she 'd break it again.

'Twas hay-making season, I can't tell the reason,
  Misfortunes will never come single, that 's plain,
For, very soon after poor Kitty's disaster,
  The devil a pitcher was whole in Coleraine.

A BALL-ROOM ROMANCE.

UNKNOWN.

FAIR good-night to thee, love,
  A fair good-night to thee,
  And pleasant be thy path, love,
Though it end not with me.
Liking light as ours, love,
  Was never meant to last;
It was a moment's fantasy,
  And as such it has passed.

We met in lighted halls,
  And our spirits took their tone,
Like other dreams of midnight
  With colder morning flown.

And thinkest thou to ever win
  A single tear from me?
Lightly won and lightly lost,
  I shed no tear for thee.

For him, the light and vain one,
  For him there never wakes
That love for which a woman's heart
  Will beat until it breaks.
And yet the spell was pleasant,
  Though it be broken now,
Like shaking down loose blossoms
  From off the careless bough.

Thy words were courtly flattery;
  Such sink like morning dew:
But ah! love takes another tone,
  The tender and the true.
There's little to remember,
  And nothing to regret:
Love touches not the flatterer,
  Love chains not the coquette.

'Twas of youth's fairy follies,
　By which no shade is cast;
One of its airy vanities,
　And like them it hath past.
No vows were ever plighted,
　We'd no farewell to say :
Gay were we when we met at first,
　And parted just as gay. . . .
A fair good-night to thee, love,
　A fair good-night awhile ;
I have no parting sighs to give,
　So take my parting smile.

"*THIRTEEN.*"

SYDNEY WALKER.

THY smiles, thy talk, thy aimless plays
　　So beautiful approve thee,
　　So winning light are all thy ways,
　I cannot choose but love thee.
Thy balmy breath upon my brow
　　Is like the summer air,
As o'er my cheek thou leanest now,
　　To plant a soft kiss there.

Thy steps are dancing toward the bound
　　Between the child and woman,
And thoughts and feelings more profound,
　　And other years are coming :

And thou shalt be more deeply fair,
　　More precious to the heart,
But never canst thou be again
　　That lovely thing thou art !

And youth shall pass, with all the brood
　　Of fancy-fed affection ;
And grief shall come with womanhood,
　　And waken cold reflection.
Thou 'lt learn to toil, and watch, and weep,
　　O'er pleasures unreturning,
Like one who wakes from pleasant sleep
　　Unto the cares of morning.

UNDER MY WINDOW.

Thomas Westwood.

UNDER my window, under my window,
   All in the midsummer weather,
   Three little girls with fluttering curls
Flit to and fro together.
There's Bell, with her bonnet of satin sheen,
And Maude, with her mantle of silver-green,
   And Kate, with the scarlet feather.

Under my window, under my window,
   Leaning stealthily over,
Merry and clear, the voice I hear
   Of each glad-hearted rover.

Ah ! sly little Kate, she steals my roses,
And Maude and Bell twine wreaths and posies,
  As busy as bees in clover.

Under my window, under my window,
  In the blue midsummer weather,
Stealing slow, on a hushed tiptoe,
  I catch them all together :
Bell, with her bonnet of satin sheen,
And Maude, with her mantle of silver-green,
  And Kate, with the scarlet feather !

Under my window, under my window,
  And off through the orchard closes,
While Maude, she flouts, and Bell, she pouts ;
  They scamper, and drop their posies :
But dear little Kate takes naught amiss,
And leaps in my arms with a loving kiss,
  And I give her all my roses.

THE PROUDEST LADY.

THOMAS WESTWOOD.

SHE Queen is proud on her throne,
　　And proud are her maids so fine;
　　But the proudest lady that ever was known
　Is this little lady of mine.
And oh! she flouts me, she flouts me!
And spurns, and scorns, and scouts me!
Though I drop on my knees, and sue for grace,
And beg and beseech, with the saddest face,
　Still ever the same she doubts me.

She is seven by the calendar,
　A lily's almost as tall;
But oh! this little lady's by far
　The proudest lady of all!

It 's her sport and pleasure to flout me!
To spurn and scorn and scout me!
But ah! I 've a notion it 's naught but play,
And that, say what she will and feign what she may,
 She can't well do without me!

For at times, like a pleasant tune,
 A sweeter mood o'ertakes her;
Oh! then she 's sunny as skies of June,
 And all her pride forsakes her.
Oh! she dances round me so fairly!
Oh! her laugh rings out so rarely!
Oh! she coaxes, and nestles, and peers, and pries,
In my puzzled face with her two great eyes,
 And owns she loves me dearly.

LITTLE BELL.

[Extract.]

THOMAS WESTWOOD.

PIPED the blackbird on the beechwood spray,
 " Pretty maid, slow wandering this way,
  What 's your name," quoth he.
" What 's your name, oh ! stop and straight unfold,
Pretty maid, with showery curls of gold."
 " Little Bell," said she.

Little Bell sat down beneath the rocks,
Tossed aside her gleaming, golden locks.
 " Bonny bird," quoth she,
" Sing me your best song, before I go."
" Here 's the very finest song I know,
 Little Bell," said he.

And the blackbird piped—you never heard
Half so gay a song from any bird;
    Full of quips and wiles,
Now so round and rich, now soft and slow,
All for love of that sweet face below,
    Dimpled o'er with smiles.

And the while that bonny bird did pour
His full heart out, freely, o'er and o'er,
    'Neath the morning skies,
In the little childish heart below
All the sweetness seemed to grow and grow,
And shine forth in happy overflow
    From the brown bright eyes.

LOVE IN A COTTAGE.

[*Extract.*]

N. P. WILLIS.

THEY may talk of love in a cottage,
And bowers of trellised vine,
Of nature bewitchingly simple,
And milkmaids half divine ;
They may talk of the pleasure of sleeping
In the shade of a spreading tree,
And a walk in the fields at morning,
By the side of a footstep free !

.   .   .   .   .

True love is at home on a carpet,
And mightily likes his ease ;
And true love has an eye for a dinner,
And starves beneath shady trees.

His wing is the fan of a lady,
   His foot's an invisible thing,
And his arrow is tipped with a jewel,
   And shot from a silver string.

TO A FISH.

JOHN WOLCOT.

WHY flyest thou away with fear?
　　Trust me there's nought of danger near,
　　　　I have no wicked hooke
All covered with a snaring bait,
Alas! to tempt thee to thy fate,
　　　　And dragge thee from the brooke.

O harmless tenant of the flood!
I do not wish to spill thy blood,
　　　　For Nature unto thee
Perchance hath given a tender wife,
And children dear, to charm thy life,
　　　　As she hath done for me.

Enjoy thy stream, O harmless fish ;
And when an angler for his dish,
    Through gluttony's vile sin,
Attempts, a wretch, to pull thee *out,*
God give thee strength, O gentle trout,
    To pull the raskall *in !*

TRANSLATIONS

FROM THE FRENCH AND GERMAN.

By ETHEL GREY.

TWENTY YEARS.

[*From the French.*]

E. BARATEAU.

THE sun had scattered each opal cloud,
  And the flowers had waked from their
    winter's rest,
The song of the skylark rang free and loud,
  And ah! there were eggs in the swallow's nest!
And for joy of the spring, that so sweet appears,
I sang with the singing of twenty years.

Out from the meadows there passed a maid,—
  How can I tell you why she was fair?
To see was to love, as she bent her head
  Over the brooklet that murmured there.

As I gazed, in an April of hopes and fears,
I dreamed with the dreaming of twenty years.

Next,—for I saw her just once again,—--
  Just once more in that rare spring-tide,—
I felt a heart-throb of a vague, sweet pain,
  For I noticed that some one was by her side !
And I turned, with a passion of sudden tears,
For they loved with the loving of twenty years.

ROSETTE.

BÉRANGER.

ES! I know you 're very fair ;
    And the rose-bloom of your cheek,
    And the gold-crown of your hair,
Seem of tender love to speak.
But to me they speak in vain,
    I am growing old, my pet,—
Ah! if I could love you now
    As I used to love Rosette !

In your carriage every day
    I can see you bow and smile ;
Lovers your least word obey,
    Mistress you of every wile.

She was poor, and went on foot,
    Badly drest, you know,—and yet,—
Ah ! if I could love you now
    As I used to love Rosette !

You are clever, and well known
    For your wit so quick and free ;—
Now, Rosette, I blush to own,
    Scarcely knew her A B C ;
But she had a potent charm
    In my youth :—ah, vain regret !
If I could but love you now
    As I used to love Rosette !

TIRESOME SPRING!

[*From the French.*]

BÉRANGER.

I HAVE watched her at her window
        Through long days of snow and wind,
    Till I learnt to love the shadow
    That would flit across her blind.
'Twixt the lime-tree's leafless branches
    In the dusk my eyes I'd strain :
Now the boughs are thick with foliage,—
    Tiresome Spring ! you've come again !

Now, behind that screen of verdure
    Is my angel lost to view ;
And no longer for the robins
    Will her white hands bread-crumbs strew.

Never in the frosts of winter,
  Did those robins beg in vain :
Now, alas ! the snow has melted,—
  Tiresome Spring ! you 've come again !

'Tis kind winter that I wish for ;—
  How I long to hear the hail
Rattling on deserted pavements,
  Dancing in the stormy gale !
For I then could see her windows,
  Watch my darling through each pane :
Now the lime-trees are in blossom,—
  Tiresome Spring ! you 've come again !

"*SHE IS SO PRETTY.*"

[*From the French.*]

Béranger.

SHE is so pretty, the girl I love,
    Her eyes are tender and deep and blue
    As the summer night in the skies above,
  As violets seen through a mist of dew.
How can I hope, then, her heart to gain?
She is so pretty, and I am so plain!

She is so pretty, so fair to see!
    Scarcely she's counted her nineteenth spring,
Fresh, and blooming, and young,—ah, me!
    Why do I thus her praises sing?
Surely from me 'tis a senseless strain,
She is so pretty, and I am so plain!

She is so pretty, so sweet and dear,
　　There 's many a lover who loves her well ;
I may not hope, I can only fear,
　　Yet shall I venture my love to tell ? . . .
Ah ! I have pleaded, and not in vain—
Though she 's so pretty, and I am so plain.

THE CRICKET ON THE HEARTH.

[Imitated from the French.]

BÉRANGER.

IN the evening, I sit near my poker and tongs,
    And I dream in the firelight's glow,
    And sometimes I quaver forgotten old songs
That I listened to long ago.
Then out of the cinders there cometh a chirp,
    Like an echoing, answering cry,—
Little we care for the outside world,
    My friend the cricket and I.

For my cricket has learnt, I am sure of it quite,
    That this earth is a silly, strange place,
And perhaps he 's been beaten and hurt in the fight,
    And perhaps he 's been passed in the race.

But I know he has found it far better to sing
    Than to talk of ill-luck and to sigh,—
Little we care for the outside world,
    My friend the cricket and I.

Perhaps he has loved, and perhaps he has lost
    And perhaps he is weary and weak,
And tired of life's torrent, so turbid and tost,
    And disposed to be mournful and meek.
Yet still I believe that he thinks it is best
    To sing, and let troubles float by,—
Little we care for the outside world,
    My friend the cricket and I.

AN INVITATION.

[*From the French.*]

Théophile Gautier.

ELL me, pretty one, where will you sail?
How shall our bark be steered, I pray?
Breezes flutter each silken vail,
Tell me, where will you go to-day?

My vessel's helm is of ivory white,
Her bulwarks glisten with jewels bright
And red gold;
The sails are made from the wings of a dove,
And the man at the wheel is the god of love,
Blythe and bold.

2 A

Where shall we sail?   'Mid the Baltic's foam?
Or over the broad Pacific roam?
   Don't refuse.
Say, shall we gather the sweet snow-flowers,
Or wander in rose-strewn Eastern bowers?
   Only choose.

"Oh, carry me then," cried the fair coquette,
"To the land where never I 've journeyed yet,
   To that shore
Where love is lasting, and change unknown,
And a man is faithful to one alone
   Evermore."

Go, seek that land for a year and a day,
At the end of the time you 'll be still far away,
   Pretty maid;—
'Tis a country unlettered in map or in chart,
'Tis a country that does not exist, sweetheart,
   I 'm afraid!

MY PRETTY NEIGHBOUR.

[*From the French.*]

Victor Hugo.

IF you 've nothing, dear, to tell me,
  Why, each morning passing by,
With your sudden smiles compel me
To adore you, then repel me,
  Pretty little neighbour, why?
Why, if you have naught to tell me,
  Do you so my patience try?

If you 've nothing, sweet, to teach me,
  Tell me why you press my hand?
I 'll attend if you 'll impeach me
Of my sins, or even preach me
  Sermons hard to understand;

But, if you have naught to teach me,
Dear, your meaning I demand !

If you wish me, love, to leave you,
Why for ever walk my way ?
Then, when gladly I receive you,
Wherefore do I seem to grieve you ?
Must I then, in truth, believe you
Wish me, darling, far away ?
Do you wish me, love, to leave you ?
Pretty little neighbour, say !

"ARISE!"

[From the French.]

VICTOR HUGO.

THE dawn has awakened the skies;
　　Closed is thy door, O my love!
　　Why not awaken, O beautiful eyes?
Blue as the heavens above.
The flowers have unfolded their leaves,
　　Wakens the rose at my feet:
Thou art a fresh budding rose,
　　Why art thou sleeping, my sweet?
Wake then, O darling, with earth's fairest things,
List to thy lover who watches and sings.

　　The world is arisen from rest,
　　　Nature around says, "Arise!"

All that is brightest and best
   Waits for its mirror—thine eyes.
Rosy clouds bring thee the day,
   " Music is here," coos the dove ;
Gifts they bring, many and rare,
   Only my heart brings thee love.
Wake then, O darling, with earth's fairest things,
List to thy lover who watches and sings.

THREE KISSES.

[Imitated from the German.]

A. von Chamisso.

YOU little maid with golden hair,
　　As at my thin grey locks you stare,
　　　　Your lisping tongue
Half asks the question which your eyes
Half mirror in their sweet surprise,
　　　　Was I once young?

Well, yes, there was a time, I think,
When even you could scarcely shrink
　　　　From saying so :
Some thought I was a handsome youth,
But then they died, in sober truth,
　　　　Long years ago.

Your dimpled face, so rosy round,
Recalls, as on my knee you bound,
     Another,
As fresh and fair, which some one wore.
Who was she?   Why, my pet, 'twas your
     Grandmother!

Once in those days I kissed her hand
(I was in love, you understand);
     She married
Your grandpapa; and as for me,
A broken heart across the sea
     I carried.

When I returned, your mother, sweet,
Was there my wearied steps to greet
     With gladness:
But then came days of lovers' tryst;
Her fair brow as a bride I kist
     In sadness.

Since then I 've travelled far and wide,
And now you 're sitting by my side,
    Her daughter !
And often from your voice they ring,
The songs your mother used to sing,—
    I taught her.

But as I kiss your baby lips,
And little rosy finger-tips,
    My laughter
Is mingled with regret : I know
The bud will to a blossom blow,
The child must to a woman grow,
    Hereafter.

A LOVE TEST.

[*Imitated from the German.*]

CARL HERLOSZSOHN.

WEET, do you ask me if you love or no?
  Soon will your answers to my questions show:
  If in your cheeks hot blushes come and go,
Like rose-leaves shaken on new-fallen snow;
If tender sorrows in your heart arise,
And sudden teardrops tremble in your eyes;
If from my presence you would sigh to part,
Believe me, darling, I have touched your heart.

If when I speak your blue-veined eyelids sink,
And veil the thoughts you scarcely dare to think;

If when I greet you, hardly you reply,
And when we part, but breathe a faint "Good-
bye!"
If your sweet face to mine you cannot raise,
Yet fear not so to meet another's gaze;
If all these things to make you glad combine,
Believe me, darling, that your heart is mine.

THE BOUQUET.

[From the German.]

UHLAND.

IF every flower's an emblem, as you say,
   And every twig suggests a separate feeling;
If sadness crouches 'neath the cypress grey,
   And love from out a rosebud may be stealing;
If colours, too, express one's state of mind,
   And Nature's tints can speak of human passion;
If Hope's fair livery in green we find,
   And Jealousy brings yellow into fashion;
Then, sweetheart, in my garden there shall blow
   All kinds of plants, whose various hues I'll borrow
In giving one bouquet to you, to show
   Yours are my love, my cares, my hopes, my sorrow.

THE MISTAKEN MOTH.

[*Imitated from the German.*]

WEGENER.

'MID the summer flush of roses
    Red and white,
Sat a damsel fair, a very
    Pretty sight;
Till a butterfly, so smart,
With a flutter and a dart,
Kissed her mouth, and made her start
    In a fright.

" Ah, forgive me !" begged the insect,
    " If you please;
I assure you that I didn't
    Mean to tease.

I but took your rosebud lip
For the rose wherein I dip,
All its honey sweet to sip
　　At mine ease."

Said the beauty, to the moth,
　　" You may try
To excuse your forward conduct,
　　Sir, but I
Wish it clearly understood
That such roses are too good
To be kissed by every rude
　　Butterfly ! "

PRINTED BY BALLANTYNE AND COMPANY
EDINBURGH AND LONDON